SBYA

FACING It

ANNE SCHRAFF

SADDLEBACK
PUBLISHING

URBAN UNDERGROUND ®

SADDLEBACK
P U B L I S H I N G
www.sdlback.com

© **2013 by Saddleback Educational Publishing**
All rights reserved. No part of this book may be reproduced in any form or by any means, electronic or mechanical, including photocopying, recording, scanning, or by any information storage and retrieval system, without the written permission of the publisher. SADDLEBACK EDUCATIONAL PUBLISHING and any associated logos are trademarks and/or registered trademarks of Saddleback Educational Publishing.

ISBN-13: 978-1-62250-045-1
ISBN-10: 1-62250-045-8
eBook: 978-1-61247-703-9

Printed in Guangzhou, China
NOR/0313/CA21300355

17 16 15 14 13   1 2 3 4 5

CHAPTER ONE

You free Sunday afternoon?" seventeen-year-old Jaris Spain asked his girlfriend, Sereeta Prince. They were both seniors at Harriet Tubman High School. "They got a cool street fair going across town. Lotsa little alt bands and great food. Somebody told me they got hot dogs to die for. And the bands are good too. Nobody famous but talented little groups at the edge of what's hap'nin'."

"Sure," Sereeta responded. "Grandma's gonna be busy. Her old friend from high school, believe it or not, is coming to visit from Alabama. They're gonna hang out." Both Sereeta's parents were divorced and remarried, and she had gone through a lot. Now she lived with her grandmother,

1

Bessie Prince. Life was more serene with her grandma.

"There's one band you gotta see, Sereeta," Jaris went on. "They started out with these two guys, one on guitar and the other on drums. They sang too, but they were kinda lame. Now they got a new singer who really rocks. It's, like, unbelievable."

Sereeta smiled. She was one of the most beautiful girls at Tubman High. Jaris had loved her since middle school, but he had won her over only in his junior year.

"By the way, Jaris," she asked him, "when are you gonna find out if that story you entered in the English contest won anything? What's it called—'Rings of Saturn'?"

"Yeah," Jaris replied, grinning sheepishly. "The more I think about it, the more I think I never even should've entered the contest. Lotsa seniors can write better stuff than me. But, anyway, next week they announce the winners."

When Jaris had first entered his story in the contest, he thought even winning honorable mention would boost his spirits. The top prize in the contest was one thousand dollars, and the second prize was five hundred. Jaris thought if he won third prize of two hundred and fifty dollars, he'd be on top of the world. Even if he only won one of the three honorable mentions, which just came with a certificate, that would be good.

But the more he thought about it, the less he believed in his story. Self-doubt was typical of him. Jaris often sank into pits of self-doubt. His father was the same way. The darkness seemed always close by, ready to engulf him, telling him he wouldn't succeed at anything.

"I wish I knew what your story was about," Sereeta said.

"It's bad luck to talk about a story before it's judged," Jaris responded. "I read that somewhere. I got enough bad karma—or whatever—just thinking about it."

Sereeta looked at the tall, handsome, dark-eyed senior she had come to love. "Babe, why are you so downbeat?" she asked.

"Oh, just little things," Jaris shrugged. "You know me. I'm like my pop, always doing the 'what-if' game. Pop's doing great since he bought the garage from old Jackson. But now he needs to spend a lot of money putting in new equipment so that he can keep on doing smog checks. The smog-check business really brings in new customers for other things. But Mom goes ballistic when he talks about spending more money on up-keep. She never liked putting the mortgage on the house to buy the garage in the first place. Lately they've been arguing. Mom thinks Pop should just drop the smog business."

"Well," Sereeta declared, "maybe going to the street fair is just what you need. It'll get your mind off that stuff. I can't wait to hear this guy you say is so good."

Jaris grinned as he responded to Sereeta. "You won't believe it when you see him, Sereeta. He's got dreadlocks, and he wears this leather vest and no shirt. He's well built, and he wears just the vest. The chicks go crazy."

"Oh, my!" Sereeta laughed. "That sounds exciting."

"I think this dude is just what the band needs to break out of so-so success and maybe land a recording contract," Jaris remarked.

"What's the guy's name?" Sereeta asked.

"He's got this one name—Antar. It's a stage name," Jaris replied.

"Jaris, you have a funny look on your face," Sereeta noted, staring at him intently. "Why do I get the feeling you're hiding something about this guy?"

"Sereeta, would I do that?" Jaris asked, putting on a fake hurt-feelings look.

Sunday dawned cool and sunny, a perfect day for a street fair. Jaris picked up Sereeta at her grandmother's house in the used Ford Focus he'd just bought. Several of the small downtown communities held street fairs, but the one on Pueblo Street was the best. It attracted bands on the verge of success, and a couple of them had gone on to national recognition. The Pueblo Street fair also had legendary food.

Jaris wore jeans and a T-shirt, and Sereeta looked stunning in a red-striped tank top and torn jeans. They walked past craft booths that Sereeta loved and that bored Jaris. Then they wandered over to where the bands were setting up.

"Oh, there's the band that Oliver Randall likes so much," Sereeta pointed. "Life of Amphibians."

Oliver Randall had become Jaris and Sereeta's close friend since coming to Tubman last year. He dated Alonee Lennox, one of Jaris's best old friends. Oliver's father was a seventy-year-old astronomy professor at the community college, and his mother was an opera singer.

"I'm surprised Oliver and Alonee aren't here," Sereeta remarked.

"Maybe they'll show up," Jaris said.

Life of Amphibians consisted of a white guy named Todd, who had red hair and a red beard, and a black guy named Rex. Rex had a shaved head and lots of earrings, nose rings, and a lip ring. They were both good on the guitar and drums. They'd been together since they had started out as a teenaged garage band about four years ago. Both guys were twenty-two years old.

"So, Jaris," Sereeta asked, "where's that band with Antar in it that you were so anxious for me to see?"

"You're looking at it, babe," Jaris answered.

"You mean Antar is with Life of Amphibians?" Sereeta responded. "Oh, wow! I bet Oliver's excited about that. He wants those guys to succeed so bad. If they got a hot new singer, he'll be thrilled."

"Yeah," Jaris agreed. "The new guy brings an awesome vitality to the band. You can just feel the excitement."

The crowd was swelling in front of the Life of Amphibians' spot. Word had already got around that Antar was with them today.

"I guess I'm out of the loop, Jaris," Sereeta commented. "The buzz is really strong around here, and I've never even heard of Antar. Where do you find this stuff out?"

"I have my sources," Jaris replied. By now, Jaris had a funny look on his face.

Rex and Todd started playing, and the music built to a crescendo. Suddenly somebody else was on stage, cradling a guitar in his muscular arms. His back was to the crowd. He was tall, with dreadlocks. When he began to sing, his voice was like rolling thunder. As he turned slowly to face the audience, the girls in the crowd began to scream. The young man flashed a smile, dazzling white in his dark face. He was handsome and electrifying as he seized the lyrics of well-known rock classics and made them his own. His voice soared with heart-wrenching emotion, then sank to a mournful moan. He moved around the stage like a wildcat, turning, twisting, kneeling on one knee, and then jumping up to do a guitar solo.

"Jaris!" Sereeta gasped. "You tricked me!"

"What?" Jaris asked, an innocent look on his smiling face.

"It's Oliver! It's Oliver Randall! Oh, Jaris—he's so . . . so *good*!" Sereeta exclaimed. "Oh my gosh! I knew he had a beautiful voice when he sang at the talent show last year, but . . ."

Jaris was shaking with laughter.

Sereeta gave him a mock punch in the chest. "You!"

"I just found out myself last week, Sereeta," Jaris explained. "I couldn't believe it when I first heard him at a little club downtown. Then I heard he was gonna be at the street fair. I just couldn't resist getting you down here. He calls himself Antar after some old African poet from over a thousand years ago. He's amazing, huh? He has such a great voice. He could do opera if he wanted, but he can really rock!"

The applause was deafening. It seemed that everyone at the street fair had gathered at this stage. Oliver sang alternative rock and reggae, and then he launched into hip-hop, raising the noise level to a roar.

When Oliver finally left the stage, Sereeta said to Jaris, "Alonee never mentioned this, even at our lunch breaks."

Every day at lunchtime, a little group of friends ate their lunches in a special spot under the eucalyptus trees. The group was nicknamed "Alonee's posse" because she brought them together. Trevor Jenkins, Jaris's best friend, was in the group. So were Kevin Walker and Derrick Shaw, among others. All the guys sat with their girlfriends. Oliver Randall was there too with Alonee, but she didn't say a word. Nor did he.

Jaris shrugged. "Oliver didn't even tell Alonee until a couple days ago, and when he did tell her, she didn't like it much," Jaris explained.

"Didn't like that he didn't tell her or didn't like it, period?" Sereeta asked.

"Both," Jaris answered. "You can't blame the chick, Sereeta. She's gotten to know this steady, dependable guy who makes good grades. He's . . . you know, *normal*. Now he's turned into some strange new persona, Antar the rocker. It's like he morphed into a whole other person."

"Yeah," Sereeta agreed. "But what's amazing is that he's so good. It just gave me chills listening to him."

"Oliver told me he just wants to help his friends, Rex and Todd," Jaris said. "You know, help them get their careers off the ground. He's willing to do anything to give them a leg up in the business, to get some buzz going about the band. But this whole deal is bound to affect him, Sereeta. Look at him up there signing autographs."

"Poor Alonee!" Sereeta sighed. "Jaris, if you were up there, surrounded by pretty, hysterical girls pawing at you, my day would be ruined."

"If I was up there singing, Sereeta," Jaris chuckled, "I'd ruin *everybody*'s day! They wouldn't be asking me for my autograph. They'd be arresting me for audience abuse."

11

"Jaris, look, there's Marko and Jasmine!" Sereeta pointed. "Wow, look at Jasmine! She's almost swooning. Oh my gosh! Look at Marko! He's having a fit." Sereeta giggled.

Oliver was offstage now, and the crowd broke up.

Marko and Jasmine joined Jaris and Sereeta. Marko fumed, "You guys see that freakin' fool up there? I couldn't believe it. Somebody at school said Oliver Randall's gone crazy and was singin' at the street fair with this stupid band. I go 'No way! That dude doesn't do rock.' Yeah, he sang ballads last year at the talent show. But that freak, now he's got dreadlocks on, and he's actin' like Lil Wayne! What's with the dude?"

"Oh, Marko," Jasmine cooed, a dreamy smile on her face. "Don't act like that. He was wonderful. That boy has real talent. Didn't you think he was just amazing, Sereeta? Didn't he send chills up your spine, girl?"

"Uh, yeah, he's good all right," Sereeta agreed.

12

Marko looked at Jaris, "Man, you better watch that chick of yours too. It ain't only Jasmine. That freakin' fool's gonna be luring all the chicks away from their guys."

Jaris was laughing so hard, he could hardly speak. "Cool it, dude. Sereeta's not going anywhere, and neither is Jasmine. They just liked the guy on stage. When you see a pretty babe singing on the stage, Marko, she gets to you, right? Don't mean you're going chasing after her. Oliver was just performing, that's all. It's nothing personal."

"Ohhh! But he has such a body," Jasmine groaned. "Those ripplin' muscles and that cool vest showin' just enough. He's really put together, that boy is. And he can sing. Oh boy, he can sing like I never heard before. He rocks me to my soul!"

Jaris could see that Jasmine was trying to make Marko jealous. She was smirking.

Marko looked at Jaris. "Man, you listening to this? Jasmine, she's goin' crazy over the fool. Sereeta too, probably. Only she got

13

sense enough to keep it to herself. But they'd both like to chase after Randall and leave us in their dust. How come Alonee's lettin' him get away with this? Can't she keep her man any better than this?"

Oliver appeared from behind the stage, dressed in a white T-shirt and jeans. He was done performing for the day. He saw the Tubman students standing together, and he came over. "Well, how'd I do?" he asked cheerfully.

"You were great, man," Jaris told him. "I never dreamed you could sing like that."

"Yeah, you were really good, Oliver," Sereeta added. "I was absolutely shocked. I knew you had a good voice, but what a performance!"

"Oliver," Jasmine said, "you blew me away."

"Lissen up, fool," Marko cut into the praise. "Waddya doin' this for? What's goin' on here, tell me that. It's a joke, right? You come on today as a joke, right? And what about that hair? Are you crazy?

Dreadlocks! You think you're Lil Wayne or somethin'?"

Oliver laughed. He poked a thumb at Marko as he spoke to Jaris. "And this from the dude who thought I was a Martian when I first showed up at Tubman, remember? He thought my skin looked too smooth. I must've got off a UFO."

Then he turned his head to speak to Marko. "No, Marko, I don't think I'm Lil Wayne. That would be very arrogant of me. Weezy is one of a kind. But a lotta guys wear their hair in dreadlocks, and it wasn't a joke. My friends in the band, they haven't got their groove yet, and I'm trying to help them."

Oliver could see that Marko wasn't getting it. Oliver tried to explain. "We figured if I joined them for a while, I could give them a boost. I signed on with them for nothing 'cause they can't afford a singer. We want to create some excitement for Life of Amphibians, maybe get a producer interested."

15

"Lissen, dude," Marko stormed. "You think Alonee's gonna stand for this, all those stupid chicks droolin' over you? You're stickin' your finger in Alonee's eye, you know that? That a way to treat your chick, man? I thought you had more class than that."

"Marko," Oliver sighed, "Alonee's a smart girl. She understands what we're doing here. She knows I go way back with Todd and Rex. They're both married guys, and they got babies. They need regular money. Lotsa good bands just perform at the street-fair level forever, and they never make a living. I don't want that to happen to them."

"And what's with the no-shirt deal, man?" Marko growled. "You up there with a lotta skin showin'. That's not cool."

"*I* think it's super cool," Jasmine remarked. She was still trying to get Marko jealous.

"I had a vest on, man," Oliver objected. "Even the country-western guys dress like I was up there."

"Come on, Jasmine," Marko commanded, "we're gettin' outta here. I'm sick

16

of talkin' to this fool." He grabbed Jasmine's hand and pulled her after him. Jasmine looked back and smiled at Oliver.

When Marko was gone, Jaris asked Oliver, "You gonna be wearing those dreadlocks at school?"

"No way," Oliver replied. "It's a wig. It's a part of my costume."

"Oliver, what's with the name Antar?" Sereeta asked. "Where'd you get it?"

"You know, I got Langston Myers, our English teacher, to thank for that," Oliver answered. "You know how big he is on African culture. Some kids think he does too much. For me, though, it's fine. We went too long without hearing anything about our culture. So maybe a little overkill is good now."

Oliver started to walk toward the food booths, and Jaris and Sereeta followed along. "Anyway," Oliver went on, "Myers told me about this dude Antar. He was a warrior and a storyteller. His mother was a slave, and his dad was a warrior and a

17

prince. Antar fell in love with this beautiful chick Abla, and he wrote poems to her. He won her over, and he kept on writing these great poems about courage, pride, and love. He eventually died in battle as a hero. I thought it'd be cool to take his name."

"So this gig today, Oliver," Jaris asked, "is this the last we see of Antar? Or are we watching the birth of a star?"

"Neither," Oliver answered, laughing again. "I'll give my friends as much time as I can fit into my schedule, what with school and stuff. I'm doing a beach concert next weekend at the place where they build sand castles. Like here—crafts, food, music. Maybe somebody'll notice us, and Life of Amphibians will take off. Anyway, right now I'm starved. They're supposed to have amazing orange chicken somewhere around here."

They found the food booth and bought heaping plates of orange chicken. They took the chicken and sodas to one of the tables.

"Hey, man!" A guy about thirty with a goatee approached Oliver. "What's the scoop on you?"

Oliver looked at the man. "Who wants to know?" he asked.

"I do the entertainment column in *Scavenger Hunt*," the man answered. "You probably seen the magazine. A thousand pages of ads and a coupla articles. It's a freebie about what's hap'nin'. Your set was pretty awesome, man. So who are you?"

"I'm Oliver Randall, a senior at Tubman High School," Oliver replied. "I use the name Antar with the band."

The goateed man stuck out his hand for a handshake. "Atticus Bowles. I got some shots of you while you were performing. I'd like to put them in the magazine and online. Could you get your parents to sign a release and e-mail it to me? We do a review and the pictures. It can't hurt you."

"Cool," Oliver agreed, shaking Bowles's hand. "Be sure to mention my band, Life of Amphibians."

"E-mail me their name, the names of the other guys and addresses, phone numbers, e-mail addresses—the works," Bowles said. "You got a website?"

"Yeah, the band's on Facebook," Oliver answered.

"Okay, dude, I'll be waiting for your e-mail," Bowles said. "Check us out online at scavengerhunt.com."

Atticus Bowles handed Oliver his business card and said, "You're pretty amazing, kid."

Jaris whistled as the man walked away. "Oliver, I'm getting the feeling something big is underway."

Oliver shrugged and explained, "No big deal. *Scavenger Hunt* is just a rag. It's filled with blurbs about so-so bands and musicians, has-beens, and never-weres. But it should be fun to check it out."

"What does your father think about all this?" Sereeta asked.

"My father's a great guy, but he doesn't get it," Oliver answered. "He looks at me with my wig and the vest and shakes his head. He goes, 'If you wanted a musical career, son, why didn't you talk to your mother?' I don't know. I feel wacky. I feel like I climbed on a roller coaster just for laughs. Now it won't stop and let me off."

"You *want* to get off?" Jaris asked.

Oliver looked right at Jaris and replied, "You know what, man? I don't know."

They finished their chicken, and Oliver left for home. As Jaris and Sereeta walked to the car, Sereeta held tightly to Jaris's hand.

"I hope he knows what he wants, Jaris," she said. "He's just about the nicest guy I know, present company excluded."

They both had the same unspoken thought: the only way the band would get a big-time contract is if Oliver stuck with it.

CHAPTER TWO

At school on Monday, Jaris met Kevin Walker in front of the large statue of Harriet Tubman. Jaris was the assistant manager at the Chicken Shack, and he had just hired Kevin. Kevin had needed a job bad when the pizza place where he worked went bust. Jaris's boss, Neal, had given a thumbs-up on Kevin.

"Hey, Kevin!" Jaris hailed. "Neal said you're doing great on the job. He said I'm a pretty good assistant manager to have hired two hotshots, you and Amberlynn Parson. Neal said so far I'm batting a thousand. Thanks for making me look good, bro."

"I'm glad," Kevin responded. "I won't disappoint you, man. You threw me a life preserver when I was goin' down. I needed a vote of confidence, and you gave it to me."

The two boys headed slowly toward the school building. "Hey," Kevin commented, "Marko Lane's telling everybody that our buddy Oliver Randall has lost his mind. He's sayin' Oliver was down at the street fair on Pueblo doin' a strip tease. He was singin' and strippin'."

Jaris laughed. "Me and Sereeta saw him. He's singing with this band, Life of Amphibians. He's been friends with those guys for a long time. The band is sorta stuck in a rut. Oliver joined them as a singer to hopefully get some buzz going."

Jaris saw Alonee Lenox and Sami Archer approaching. They stopped to wait for them. "Kevin," Jaris said, "he's awfully good. The chicks were really freakin' out. That's what got Marko mad. Oliver had his hair in this dreadlocks wig, and he's shirtless except for a vest. The chicks didn't mind that one bit. Jasmine was really enjoying it." Jaris chuckled. "She had Marko doing a slow burn."

"Yeah? Oliver has good pipes, that's for sure," Kevin agreed. "I'm not surprised he can belt out rock and roll."

"He was doing rock, reggae, hip-hop, even a little country," Jaris responded. "Then this dude from *Scavenger Hunt* comes along. He's doing a piece on him in the magazine and online. I think even Oliver was a little surprised at the buzz."

"I saw them on Facebook," Kevin noted. "They're edgy. Hey, that's not bad. Good for Oliver. He's a good guy and he deserves it."

By this time, Alonee and Sami had caught up with the boys.

"You guys," Sami Archer exclaimed, "everybody talkin' 'bout Antar. I could kick myself that I missed the boy yesterday. They sayin' there were hot sparks flyin' off that boy's leather vest." Sami was a beautiful full-figured girl who was best friends with everybody in Alonee's posse. No one was more loved and trusted than Sami.

"Don't worry, Sami," Jaris told her. "He'll be back with the band next Sunday at Sand Castle Beach."

Jaris glanced a little nervously at Alonee, who was Oliver's girlfriend. They were very close. She had a faint smile on her face, but she didn't look very happy.

"I remember Oliver singing at some beach talent show when we first dated," Alonee recalled. "He has such a great voice. He did some beautiful ballads at the junior talent show here at school last year too. I caught his Antar act, and I was shocked. I mean, yeah, he can rock. I guess Oliver can do just about anything he puts his mind to. But seeing him dressed like that and gyrating around with those flying dreadlocks—wow!"

"Don't worry, girl," Sami said. "It's just something he's doin' to help those dudes in the band. They kinda lame. They play good guitar and drums, but they nothin' special.

Y'hear what I'm sayin'? Oliver told me the black dude in the band, Rex, his wife expectin' a second baby. They gotta make some money. Oliver, he just givin' them a hand up."

"It's just that he doesn't even look like himself when he's that Antar," Alonee remarked. "He looks like some strange guy I don't even know."

"Marko's tellin' everybody he's showing too much skin under that vest," Kevin commented. "I guess Jasmine's going wild over Oliver."

"Jasmine, she ain't too reliable," Sami noted. "Remember at her birthday party when that dude Zendon started croonin' to her? Next thing, she's packin' her bags to run away with 'im. 'Member? Turns out, he just murdered somebody. Goes to show the chick is flaky."

"Marko'll have to wheedle another gold chain or somethin' nice outta his father to cool Jasmine down," Kevin snorted. "That'll cool her hots for Oliver."

Everybody laughed and headed to their classes.

Later, as usual, the gang gathered for lunch under the eucalyptus trees. Alonee and Oliver showed up together, as they always did. Oliver looked like himself again in a white T-shirt and close-cropped hair.

"Everybody talkin' 'bout you, dude," Derrick advised. "Me and Destini comin' down next Sunday to Sand Castle Beach. I'm kinda scared, though. Word is you're chick bait, dude. Destini might freak on me, and I'd be awful lonely without this babe."

Oliver laughed. "It's just an act to get some buzz going for my buddies in that band. Everybody and his brother has a little garage band. It's hard to get noticed in the crowd."

"Oliver, what gave you the idea to rock like that?" Jaris asked between bites of his sandwich. "I remember you saying once that music wasn't your thing."

"Yeah," Oliver responded. "Actually, my moment of insight came last summer when Mom and Dad and I went to the Caribbean. You guys know my mom sings opera. Man, she loves it so much. It really makes her happy. She told me this past summer that I have a pretty good voice. Isn't there *something* I could do to use it?"

Oliver sipped his soda and went on. "Well, a lightbulb went off in my brain. I got this powerful voice, and a lot of rockers got thin, reedy voices. So I figured I'd be a novelty. If I put these pipes to work rocking, and well . . . I auditioned for Mom. She got a little huffy, like *what are you doing*?"

"Didn't she like your rock-and-roll singing?" Sereeta asked.

"That's an understatement, Sereeta," Oliver responded, rolling his eyes. "She thinks of me as a ballad singer. I go, 'Hey, Mom, I was born fifty years too late.' Nowadays everybody goes for rock, hip-hop, rap. You ask anybody under seventy, and they like rock. People retiring now, they grew up on rock."

28

"Do *you* like rock?" Sereeta asked.

"I could take it or leave it at first, but now it's kinda fun," Oliver admitted. "It's like going wild. It's explosive, like a blast. I think this rocker freak was always hiding inside me, and I kept him in the attic. Now he's gotten downstairs. He's got me by the throat, and he won't let go."

"You can say that again," Alonee sighed.

Oliver reached for Alonee and pulled her gently against him. "You gotta come Sunday, babe," he told her. "I got a new vest. I went into one of those old costume places, and I got this vest with rhinestones—"

"Elvis has entered the buildin'!" Sami declared.

"Oh, Oliver!" Alonee groaned. "A rhinestone vest!"

"Aw, come on, Alonee," Oliver pleaded. "It's a fun ride, but it won't be fun if you're not on it with me."

Alonee looked at Oliver and smiled. "Okay, I'll be there. But don't be angry if I pretend I don't know you. I might just hide behind one of those big beach umbrellas."

When Jaris got home from school, his parents were talking in the kitchen. Jaris stopped to listen before going any farther.

"Babe," Pop was saying, "I gotta use our line of credit to put in the new equipment. The smog deal brings in so much other business. It gets new people in. Most of the people needin' smog checks got these old beaters that need repairs too."

"Lorenzo," Mom sighed, "I just have this sinking feeling that we're going deeper in debt, and this garage of yours is going to ruin us."

"Listen, babe," Pop cajoled, "the business has doubled since Jackson sold the garage to me. I been makin' double payments on the mortgage, and it's goin' down fast. I just need this money now for the smog stuff. After that, it's clear sailin'. Babe, how 'bout if you trust your old man? Stick with me now, babe, and you won't be sorry."

"What can I say?" Mom groaned, weariness in her voice.

"You're with me then?" Pop asked.

"Haven't I always been, even against my better judgment," Mom sighed.

"You won't be sorry, babe," Pop promised.

Jaris hurried outside. He didn't want his parents to know he had overheard their conversation. As Jaris was coming in the second time, Pop met him at the door with a big smile on his face.

"Pop," he said, "you're home early. Wassup?"

"Your Mom and I had a talk," Pop explained. "We agreed to use the credit line for the smog equipment. We're good to go. I'm on the way to the bank now, get it all set up. It's gonna be great!"

Pop started whistling as he headed for his pickup truck. Jaris recalled how depressed Pop used to be when he was an auto mechanic working with the former garage owner. Then Pop borrowed the money to buy the shop. Now Jaris was amazed at how owning Spain's Auto Care had increased his confidence. He was a new man.

When Jaris went into the house, he saw his mom at the computer. "Well, Mom," he remarked, "the English department is going to announce the winners of the short story contest this Friday after classes."

Mom swung around in her chair to face Jaris. "I hope you win the top prize, honey," Mom responded. "You know, when I was in college, I sort of wanted to be a writer. I even had this fantasy that I'd write amazing books and be the girl genius of my time. A woman by the name of Alice Walker was writing amazing books then. She was celebrated all over the world, and she was sort of my hero. I thought I'd be like her. But then reality set in. I went into teaching, and I never regretted it. I really love to teach."

Mom paused then and looked at Jaris seriously. Jaris knew what was really on her mind. "You know," she began, "we're going to go deeper in debt to get that smog stuff for your father's garage. I hate that. Debt really bothers me."

"Yeah, but it'll be okay, Mom," Jaris assured her. "Pop's doing so good over there. Every time I pass the place, the cars are stacked up."

"You know, Jaris, he *always* gets his way, your father," Mom insisted. "I can talk until I'm blue in the face, but he wants what he wants. I love him dearly, Jaris, but I'm not an equal in this marriage. I suppose few women are. I make good money myself. I'm a professional, but he's the boss. Sometimes it just infuriates me. If I didn't love him so much . . ." Mom stopped short of finishing her sentence. "If I didn't love you kids so much that I want you to have a mother and father under the same roof . . ." She didn't finish this sentence either.

Jaris looked at his mother—his beautiful, angry mother—sitting there with fire in her eyes. "You know what, Mom?" Jaris told her. "I love you, Mom. That's a given.

33

But I respect you as a woman with incredible integrity and courage. I respect you so much. There's nobody in the whole world I respect more. That's why I'm gonna be a teacher too. I want to be like you."

Mom's angry expression softened. She looked shocked. Then she said in a trembling voice, "You're a lovely young man, Jaris. I'm so proud of you." The fire in her eyes dimmed and then disappeared, put out by a few tears. "I guess it's all worth it, huh?" she asked with a rueful smile.

"Yeah, Mom," Jaris responded. He walked over to his mother and kissed her cheek.

On Tuesday, a classic car show was in town, and Jaris and Kevin went to it after school. They drove in Kevin's street rod. They rode in silence for a while. Then Kevin asked Jaris a question.

"Jaris, you think if Oliver gets real hot with that gig he's doing, he'll change? I mean, there's a dude who seems almost too good to be true. What's it going to do to him if the chicks keep comin' on like they are?"

"I think he'll stay the same," Jaris responded. "He's a pretty solid guy."

Kevin went around a corner a bit too fast.

"Easy, dude!" Jaris yelled. "I don't wanna die before I find out how I did in that short story contest."

"Sorry," Kevin apologized, slowing down. "But get real, man. If dozens of hot babes were jumpin' up and down and screaming your name, wouldn't that change *you*?"

"Luckily, I'll never have to find out," Jaris said. "How about you, Kevin? Would it change you?"

"I think so, man," Kevin admitted. "I mean, I like Carissa. But if all those chicks were lining up to get my autograph, how could I get past that? Look at all the celebrities. They're splittin' up all the time. You find somebody who's famous and stickin' with one person over the long haul, they're like an oddity. It's gotta go to your head if you become, like, some idol. Even the word 'idol,' it kinda bugs me. Like an idol is something you oughta worship, man. But these famous people, I mean, the world idolizes them."

"Yeah," Jaris admitted. "I can't imagine ever not wanting to be with Sereeta. But then nobody's gonna be wanting my autograph anytime soon."

At the car show, Kevin hurried toward a 1991 Alfa Romeo Spider. It was green and tan. "Look, it's less then ten grand, man," Kevin noted.

"Hey, there's a Lincoln Continental, Kevin," Jaris pointed. "Isn't she a beauty? Costs less than my Ford Focus did. But I bet it drinks up a lotta gas. Probably a beater too. I'd spend all the money I had keeping it on the road."

The boys strolled from car to car. Kevin was wearing a T-shirt with the Tubman Track Team logo on the back. A pretty girl who had been admiring the Alfa Romeo Spider began looking at Kevin.

"Hey, dude, look at the babe checking you out," Jaris whispered.

The girl walked over to the boys. "Hi, you guys," she greeted. "You students at Tubman?"

"Yeah," Kevin replied. "Why?"

"I go to Lincoln High," the girl said. "But I saw online that a really hot new rocker goes to your school. Do you guys know Antar? He is just awesome."

Jaris and Kevin looked at each other.

"Yeah, we know him," they both answered at the same time.

"Man, you don't think you could introduce me to him, do you?" the girl asked. "I mean, they showed him online at the band's website. I downloaded some of his music, and—oh, wow!—is he really that cute?"

"Cute?" Kevin repeated the word. "He looks about the same as you saw online. At school, he skips the dreadlocks and the vest."

"What's his real name?" the girl asked. "Would you have his phone number?"

"Ummm, sorry, no," Jaris replied. Kevin shook his head no.

The girl reached in her purse and pulled out a photo of herself. She scribbled her name, Kiki Flanders, and her cell phone number on the back of the picture. "Will you give this to Antar? Tell him I'd just adore for him to call me."

Jaris looked at the photo. The girl didn't look much older than Jaris's fifteen-year-old sister, Chelsea. The encounter with the girl had started out amusing, but now Jaris was getting steamed.

"Are you a ninth-grader?" he asked her.

Kiki shrugged. "So what?" she replied.

"You got no business dating seniors. You're a kid," he snapped.

"I date older guys all the time," the girl objected.

"Well, you shouldn't," Jaris advised, turning and walking away. Kevin followed.

"I hope I never catch Chelsea passing out her picture and trying to snag a date with a senior guy," Jaris fumed. "You gotta wonder where the parents are."

Kevin grinned. "Man, you still savin' the world, Jare?"

"I don't know, maybe," Jaris admitted. "But doesn't anybody *care* about that kid?" Anger was in Jaris's voice. "Like Chelsea's friend Athena. She might as well be an orphan."

Kevin threw his arm around Jaris's shoulders. "You're beatin' your head against a brick wall, bro, but I love you for it."

CHAPTER THREE

All day Friday at Tubman High, Jaris had a hard time keeping his mind on his classes. At two thirty that afternoon, the winners in the short story contest would be announced.

When the gang went to lunch under the eucalyptus trees, Jaris was trying very hard to get the contest off his mind.

Alonee Lennox showed up for lunch, but Oliver wasn't with her. "Oliver had to go someplace," Alonee explained. "He's really busy lately with all that rehearsing for the gigs with the band and everything. Now that he's a superstar, he doesn't have time for the usual things." Alonee had a smile on her face, but it wasn't a happy smile.

There was a tinge of bitterness in Alonee's voice. Jaris hated to hear that. It was so unlike Alonee to be bitter about anything.

"This is gonna pass like everythin' else does," Sami declared encouragingly. "The boy's jus' goin' through somethin'. When he gets it outta his system, he gonna be jus' fine."

"I don't know," Derrick Shaw objected.

All eyes turned on Derrick, who had the uncanny ability to always say the wrong thing. He never meant to hurt anyone, but he sometimes did just by saying the wrong thing.

While everyone else was assuring Alonee that Oliver would soon be back to normal, Derrick picked that moment to say the wrong thing. "I think Oliver is on to something. Me and Destini goin' down there Sunday to find out if he's as good as everybody's sayin'. If he is, this just might be the beginning of a big career in show business. Seems to me like it's the real deal."

Derrick didn't catch on to the glares of everyone in the posse. He just kept rattling on. "I was workin' at the store last night. Some people who know I go to Tubman asked me if I knew Antar, and they were, like, starstruck. They got this funny look on their faces, and they go, 'You really know the guy? What's he like?' and stuff like that."

Alonee's smile faded. She sank back in the grass and stared at the passing clouds. Jaris felt so sorry for Alonee. He'd always felt close to her. They were kids together. Somewhere along the line, Alonee had even fallen in love with Jaris, but Jaris had always wanted Sereeta. Alonee never had a chance. When Oliver came along and Alonee fell for him, Jaris was delighted. But now Jaris was very upset to think that the couple might be in trouble.

Langston Myers, Jaris's English teacher, had just self-published a novel. It was on the Harlem Renaissance of the 1920s, an outpouring of African American music and art in New York City. He had been asked to speak at a symposium, so Mr. Pippin, a junior English teacher, took his class that day. Jaris had always liked Mr. Pippin, but the teacher had a terrible time keeping discipline in his classroom. Discipline was especially poor when Marko Lane and his friends disrupted classes for their own amusement.

Mr. Pippin looked wearier and more beaten down every time Jaris saw him. The teacher was a sad, stooped figure as he stood behind Mr. Myers's desk. His old and beat-up briefcase was slumped on the floor like a sick, brown beast. Jaris sympathized with the teacher. Mr. Pippin hadn't wanted to be in the classroom for many years now. He was counting the days to his retirement.

Mr. Pippin lectured about patriotic poetry. He read "In Flanders Field" by Lieutenant Colonel John McCrae. "Notice," Mr. Pippin pointed out, "how the poet describes the beautiful poppies growing on the graves of the war dead. Flanders Fields is a cemetery for the fallen soldiers. Long lines of crosses mark the graves. In the final stanza, is there a call to arms?"

Oliver Randall raised his hand. " 'Take up our quarrel with the foe,' " he quoted.

"Yes," Mr. Pippin replied. "How much more persuasive is this call coming from those who have already died in the cause? Notice he talks about throwing the torch to soldiers still alive. Then we have Oliver Wendell Holmes's 'God Save the Flag.' The flag is stained with the blood of the brave. But then there is poetry that takes an opposite position. Can anyone cite a poem that takes a view that is contrary to patriotic fervor?"

Sereeta volunteered. " 'Base Details' by Siegfried Sassoon. It's about the majors in the army who aren't getting killed while the young soldiers go into battle and die. It says, 'When the war is done and youth stone dead,' the officers are 'safe in bed.' "

Jaris half listened to the discussion. He had entered writing contests in the fifth, seventh, and eighth grades but hadn't even won an honorable mention. Jaris thought he wouldn't win anything today either. He wondered why he even entered the contest.

His story was "The Rings of Saturn." It told of an old man who had never accomplished much in life, and now he was dying. He had aspired to be an astronomer, but he never achieved that dream. The closest he came to it was saving enough money to buy a really good telescope. He worked for a furniture company, and he raised a family. On nights when he wasn't too tired, he went onto the roof of his apartment building to observe his beloved sky. Now, at the end of his life, he was alone and dying.

One night, a teenaged boy joined him on the roof, and on that night, the rings of Saturn were visible. The old man and the boy started talking. It turned out that the boy loved astronomy too, but his family couldn't afford to buy him a telescope. On impulse, the old man gave the boy his telescope. Suddenly, he felt a peace he had not known in years. He died ten days later.

Then, ten years from that day, a young astronomer visited the grave of the old man. He had just graduated from college, and he was beginning what would be an illustrious career. The young man laid a rose on the grave. In the silence of the graveyard, he whispered a thank-you. "Except for the gift of the telescope, I might have abandoned my dreams. But in the rings of Saturn, you showed me what I might be. Thank you."

Jaris thought it was a pretty good story, but the old, familiar storms of insecurity swirled in Jaris's brain. He overcame them better now than he used to. Still they came, the small taunting voices that mocked his efforts.

"Why do I do stuff like this to myself?" Jaris crossly thought to himself. "Why do I enter contests just to prove, over and over, that I can't win? If I hadn't entered the contest, I wouldn't be all nervous today waiting for the results."

Jaris didn't know anybody else who had a story entered in the contest except two people. A girl named Sandy was the top student in Mr. Myers's class, and Jaris figured she had probably written the winning entry.

If she hadn't, then Lydell Nelson did. Lydell had been keeping a diary of his tragic personal history. As a child, he witnessed the murder of his beloved father. Since then, he'd been living with relatives who treated him poorly. Jaris felt that Lydell deserved to win.

Jaris would be in his last class when the announcement was made. He didn't know many students in that class. Just as well. Trevor Jenkins, Kevin, Oliver, or Sereeta would be there to offer their condolences. Jaris could be miserable all by himself. Nothing was worse than having your well-meaning friends patting you on the back when you came up a loser.

With Mr. Myers still at the symposium, the senior member of the English department, Mr. Pippin, was going to make the announcement. At the end of the class, the teacher instructed everyone. "All students remain at your desks for the English short story announcement." Because most students didn't have a stake in the contest, they shifted restlessly, anxious to go. But Jaris sat grimly still, his fingers tightening into fists as his hands lay on his lap.

Finally, Mr. Pippin's reedy voice came over the PA system. First, he read the names of three students who had received honorable mentions and certificates of merit. Then he thanked Anson Whitaker, a local business owner, for donating the prize money.

"Oh, well," Jaris thought, "so much for an honorable mention."

"And now for the third place winner," Mr. Pippin continued as Jaris's shoulders hunched up. "Congratulations to Sandy Munn for her story, 'Goldenrod.' Sandy will be given the two-hundred-and-fifty-dollar cash award. Second-place winner and recipient of five hundred dollars is Jaris Spain for his story, 'The Rings of Saturn.'

The one-thousand-dollar award and our congratulations go to Lydell Nelson for his story, 'The Last Slice of Pie.' Thank you all for participating, and please come to my office to pick up your certificates and checks."

The PA clicked off. Kids scrambled from the desks for the classroom door, eager to start their weekend.

Jaris sat stunned at his desk. He thought he must have heard it wrong or imagined it. "Did I really just win second place and five hundred dollars?" he asked himself.

Then Jaris realized that the class had emptied out. The teacher, who was as anxious as her students to get on with her weekend, was waiting for him to leave. Jaris jumped up from his desk and hurried outside the room, where his friends were waiting for him.

"Jaris," Kevin cried, high-fiving him, "way to go, man!"

Sereeta gave Jaris a hug, and Trevor and Derrick slapped him on the back. Jaris stared at them and asked, "You sure that was my name Mr. Pippin called out?"

"Get over to the English department office, fool, and collect your loot," Kevin commanded, laughing. He gave Jaris a shove to get him on his way.

Jaris met up with Lydell Nelson coming out of Mr. Pippin's office. Jaris had never seen Lydell looking so happy. "Congratulations, dude," Jaris told him. "You the man!"

"Back at you," Lydell responded.

Mr. Pippin was sitting at his desk, his beat-up old briefcase beside his chair like a faithful old scarred dog. "Jaris," Mr. Pippin remarked, getting up with a rare smile on his face. He held out his hand. "I was delighted that you won one of the top prizes. You wrote a very fine story. I am pleased to give you this." He handed Jaris an envelope containing the five-hundred-dollar check and a certificate of merit.

"Thanks, Mr. Pippin," Jaris replied, shaking the teacher's hand. "Thanks very much."

"You earned it, Jaris," Mr. Pippin said. "It was your doing, not mine."

Jaris was filled with an overwhelming sense of gratitude to Mr. Pippin and the whole English department that chose his story. His mood shifted from dark worry to high exultation. He had expected nothing, and now he was blessed. He wanted to embrace Mr. Pippin and the other teachers.

He had a fleeting vision; he'd go out to the statue of Harriet Tubman and shout out, "Thank you, Harriet Tubman High School, for how you have honored me in this special way today. Thank you for my fine teachers and for all the wonderful experiences I've had here. Thank you for our spot under the eucalyptus trees that sheltered me and my friends. Thank you!"

"Jaris," Mr. Pippin said, yanking Jaris back into the moment. "I think you know that you have always been one of my favorite students. You have been one of the rare students who made my ordeal here bearable. I wouldn't say this to just anyone,

Jaris, but I will say it to you. You and a few others have enabled me to go on teaching when I was totally exhausted in mind and spirit. You cannot imagine the times you lifted me up with a thoughtful question or a good comment."

"I enjoyed your class, Mr. Pippin." That was all Jaris could say, amazed that the teacher was opening up as he was. "I learned a lot from you."

Mr. Pippin seemed eager to unburden himself. "There was one time—I doubt you even remember it. We had a guest speaker that day, a colleague of mine from earlier days. He was a lovely man, but one not used to today's teenagers. He worked for the mayor. The Lane boy was sitting up front that day. He began discussing his duties. Marko Lane thrust out those great arms of his into the air and made loud yawning sounds, right in the face of this poor man. I was mortified."

Mr. Pippin shook his head in sad remembrance. "My guest was crushed," he went on. "I asked the class if anyone had any questions to ask our guest, and for a moment there was dead silence. I thought that forty-eight minutes of torment lay ahead. And then you began to ask the man what the most important problems facing the city were, in his opinion."

Jaris smiled. "Yeah, I remember, Mr. Freulich," he said.

"Yes, and Mr. Freulich then came to life," Mr. Pippin responded, smiling. "As you continued to ask interesting questions, you saved the class. I knew full well that you couldn't have cared less about the answers to your questions, but you asked them in order *to help me . . . to help that poor man.* I thought, 'What a marvelous young man to rise to the occasion like that.' Mr. Freulich died this past spring, and in the last conversation I had with him, he mentioned that day—and *you.*"

Jaris and Mr. Pippin shook hands, and Jaris left the building, clutching his envelope.

Sereeta had been standing outside waiting for him. She bobbed up and down a couple of times, squealing, and then flew into his arms, hugging him.

"I'm so proud of you, Jaris!" she cried. "The three winning stories are gonna be in the school newspaper! I can finally read yours there or online at Tubman's website."

"Babe," Jaris chuckled, "you don't know what that means to me. I mean, that you can be that so proud of me when I don't even wear a vest or dreadlocks!"

"It's okay if you ever want to, though, Jaris," Sereeta giggled. "You'd look amazing in a vest and—"

"No way, babe!" Jaris checked his watch. "Hey, I don't report to the Chicken Shack for two hours. What do you say we go down to the bay and watch the sun go down? We'll grab some mochas."

"You're on," Sereeta said.

They drove down to the bay, got some mochas, and parked the Ford Focus at the top of a bluff. They walked carefully down a little trail to a place in the sand. Jaris spread an old towel he kept in the car, and they sat down. The surf was up because of an offshore storm. After a few minutes of surf watching, Sereeta spoke.

"Jaris," she began, "I'm getting all kinds of e-mails and text messages from my father. He came down here for that one day and spent the whole time talking about his stepkids. Then he skulked away in the night. And now he's saying stuff like, 'Didn't we have a wonderful time?' "

Sereeta smiled a cold smile before going on. "I just have to laugh. Jaris, I cried at the time. It hurt that he wasn't interested in me when we hadn't seen each other in three years. But now I'm okay. I can even laugh about it. Me and Mom are getting closer all the time. We hang with little Jake, and it's pretty cool having a baby brother. And best of all, Jaris, you fill my life with so much happiness that nothing can really hurt me."

They lay back on the towel as the surf crashed. Sheets of foamy seawater rushed to within a few feet of their towel. Jaris and Sereeta held each other, kissing for a long time. Jaris felt so happy. The day had been so wonderful, and now he was alone with his girl. For now, all the darkness that had ever threatened him was gone. They were bathed in the warm, healing light.

Later, Jaris took Sereeta home to her grandmother's house. Then he headed for the Chicken Shack for his night shift. At the store, Trevor gave him a bear hug. "When they announced you got second place, man, I went crazy!" Trevor told him. "Boy, you deserved it."

"Thanks, Trev," Jaris responded, getting into his yellow and white Chicken Shack shirt. "I was amazed when I won. I woulda been happy with one of the honorable mentions. I called Pop at the garage. I think the whole neighborhood heard him yelling. Then I called Mom. Chelsea was home, and she screamed, and I think Mom was crying."

Jaris tucked in his shirt and faced Trevor before going to the front of the store. "Winning that contest's second place, Trev," he said, "it's like a sign that I'm on the right track. That going for being a teacher and writing on the side is gonna be right for me. I was pretty sure that's where I wanted to go, but this kinda sealed the deal. It's like you see a path ahead, and you're pretty sure it's the right one. Then your dog runs ahead of you down that path, and all of a sudden you're sure."

Kevin was already there, wearing his Chicken Shack shirt with the rooster on the back. "Behold the scribe!" Kevin declared. "What hath thee to say to us peons?"

"Knock it off, dude," Jaris replied, laughing.

"Forsooth!" Kevin exclaimed.

"I'm gonna pelt you with these spicy chicken wings in a minute, man," Jaris threatened.

CHAPTER FOUR

After the shift ended, Jaris and Kevin were outside standing next to Kevin's street rod.

"Gotta take this beater in to your pop tomorrow," Kevin said. "Not a bad leak so far, but I think I need a new radiator."

"Pop'll give you a good deal, Kevin," Jaris told him. "And listen, I'll loan you some money if you need it. I'm rich. I just won five hundred bucks."

"Thanks but no thanks, man," Kevin responded. "You've done enough for me. I can handle it."

Kevin's cell phone rang. The second he heard the caller, he looked upset. "It's Cory Yates—" he said to Jaris while listening.

"You still friends with that bum?" Jaris asked, frowning.

"Shut up, Jaris!" Kevin snapped. He listened for a few minutes before shutting the phone. "Bad news," Kevin reported, shaking his head. "You know Cory's brother, Brandon, and Shane Burgess? They were in the slammer for selling drugs. Well, they both broke out last night."

Jaris felt numb. Shane Burgess was the younger brother of Ms. Torie McDowell, Jaris's favorite teacher at Tubman. Everyone at school loved her. She taught history, and right now Jaris was taking AP American History with her. Ms. McDowell came from a messed-up family. She had managed to lift herself out of the drug-infested disaster, but her younger brother, Shane, couldn't. Ms. McDowell had tried desperately to rescue Shane from the streets, where he belonged to a gang—the Nite Ryders—and dealt drugs.

One night, Brandon and Shane were cutting a deal for crack cocaine with Zendon Corman on Grant Street—part of a rough neighborhood. At the same time, Zendon shot his cousin dead. The two young men almost got caught up in a murder rap, but they dodged that. Now Zendon was going on trial for murder, and they were doing time for dealing in drugs. Ms. McDowell was brokenhearted when Shane got into that serious trouble. Now things were even worse for him.

Kevin explained. "The cops checked Cory out. Thought the guys were with him, but Cory hasn't seen them. All he knows is that they busted out of jail, and now they're on the loose."

"Oh man, ugh!" Jaris groaned. "Poor Ms. McDowell. She's gotta be sick about this. She tried so hard to help that kid. For a while there, he seemed to be doing good. He was staying clean and living with his sister."

Jaris stared at the ground in disbelief. "I talked to him just before he got into that trouble," Jaris continued. "He was excited about playing baseball again. He used to be a really good player. They nicknamed him 'Sparky.' This is just so bad, Kev. Nobody ever tried harder than Ms. McDowell to save somebody, and now . . ."

Kevin shook his head. "Drugs are a deep, dark hole, man. Doin' them is like falling into a well. No matter how hard you try, you can't get up those slippery walls. My mom used to talk to me about drugs. She made me swear to her I'd never even smoke weed. When she was dyin', she made me swear it. I did swear, and I'll never break that promise. I don't know where she is, but she knows what I'm doin'. And I'm not about to break my promise."

The boys went their separate ways. Jaris went home. The beautiful day, he felt, had turned dark. He never had a teacher he liked and respected as much as Ms. McDowell. She was not only an excellent teacher, but when any kid needed help, she was there for that student. It seemed so wrong that this was happening to her.

On Sunday, Jaris picked up Sereeta and headed for Sand Castle Beach to hear Oliver perform with Life of Amphibians again.

On the drive there, Jaris told Sereeta about Shane Burgess and Brandon Yates breaking out of jail.

"Oh!" Sereeta sighed. "That's so sad. I'm so sorry to hear that."

Once, when Sereeta was in a very low point in her life, a long talk with Ms. McDowell had gotten her back on track. Ms. McDowell had shared her own struggle—a life with parents on drugs and siblings who had to raise themselves. Sereeta's pain of going through her parents' divorce and their abandonment of her seemed not so overwhelming. Sereeta was moved by Ms. McDowell's willingness to share her story and by her courage. The girl found the strength to fight her own demons. She would be forever grateful to the teacher.

"Do you think he'll go to Ms. McDowell and try to get help from her?" Sereeta asked. "That would put her in a terrible spot. He's an escaped criminal, and yet he's her little brother. She might be tempted to hide him."

"She can't help him like that, Sereeta," Jaris responded. "She'd only get into serious trouble herself. I just hope those guys have the sense to turn themselves in before they get in even deeper."

At the beach it was pleasantly warm, sort of an Indian summer day. The water had grown too cold for swimming. But plenty of people were strolling on the sand and at the craft and food booths. Most of the people were milling around where the bands were setting up.

Jaris and Sereeta got ice cream cones and waited where Oliver and his friends were tuning up.

Jaris recognized a lot of other kids from Tubman High waiting for Life of Amphibians to perform. Everybody knew Oliver Randall would be fronting for the band as Antar. That was what they came to see and hear. Derrick Shaw and Destini Fletcher came with Sami Archer and Matson Malloy. Kevin and Carissa were there, and Marko Lane and Jasmine joined them.

Jaris could see that Marko didn't want to be there. This was the last place on earth he wanted to be, but Jasmine had insisted. Marko figured he better come. He had to keep his eye on Jasmine when she started freaking out over Antar with the other crazy chicks. Jaris heard them arguing before Jasmine left to buy sandwiches. Jaris walked over to Marko.

"Lissen, dude," Jaris advised, "here's some advice. Don't get so worked up over this. Be cool. That'll sit a lot better with Jasmine. Show her you trust her."

"Yeah, but I *don't* trust her," Marko objected. "She's a crazy chick, or she wouldn't have tried to run off with Zendon that time. You're lucky, Jaris. Jasmine ain't like Sereeta. You got a solid chick there. I got a loose cannon, y'hear what I'm sayin'?"

"Not to worry," Jaris insisted. "Zendon, he was deliberately coming on to Jasmine. He was playing on her fantasies. Oliver won't be doing that. He won't get personal with any of the chicks. You know that. He's not into stuff like that. You got nothing to worry about. It's like going to a rock concert. Your chick goes gaga over some rock idol, but he's outta reach."

Marko seemed slightly consoled by what Jaris said.

Antar stepped out on stage in front of the Life of Amphibians band. He was shirtless as before, but he wore the rhinestone-studded vest. He skipped the dreadlocks in favor of a mop of dark curly hair.

Antar's booming voice soared through a variety of rhythm and blues and rock hits. He did "Icky Thump" from the White Stripes and mixed Bruce Springsteen songs with Foo Fighter hits. In a tribute to Michael Jackson, he wailed out a haunting bit from the *Thriller* album. Oliver seemed to be having a ball. He was grinning one minute and looking grim and serious the next. He sprinted around the stage, holding his guitar against his chest.

Between numbers, the applause and screams from the crowd were deafening.

Jaris watched the girls from Lincoln High and Tubman High cheering and squealing.

"He's really wonderful!" Sereeta commented.

"You know what, Sereeta?" Jaris wondered. "If this guy takes off, is he gonna want to go to college and become a scientist or something? I don't see it. I just don't see it."

Jaris hadn't seen Alonee Lennox arrive. But there she was, standing behind Jaris and Sereeta.

"Hey, Alonee," Jaris said sheepishly. "He's, uh, something else, isn't he?" Jaris hoped she hadn't heard what he had just said. Alonee looked sour. She and Oliver had arrived together at Sand Castle Beach that morning. But he soon left to get ready for his gig, and she'd been visiting the craft booths.

"You're right, Jaris," Alonee agreed grimly. "This stuff changes a person completely. No way is Oliver gonna be happy going to a boring old university and all that.

Not when he could be traipsing around the country—and maybe the world—in his rhinestone vest and crazy hairstyles. Just listen to that applause. I mean, if he hits it big with this band, he's not gonna want to leave it. Todd and Rex are good, but without Oliver, they'd just sink like a stone again. Oliver isn't going to leave them in the lurch. And why should he walk away himself from something so . . . so exciting?"

Sereeta felt sorry for Alonee. Sereeta could only imagine how she would feel if Jaris was in Oliver's spot. What if Jaris were up on stage, prancing around in a rhinestone vest with the girls squealing and jumping up and down?

But Sereeta could sympathize with Oliver too. Oliver had grown up with a diva mom, who told him of her own joy as she traveled the world singing in operas. Music was the delight of her life. She often regaled Oliver with stories from her happy career. Oliver's mother had planted a seed. Her path in life was more enchanting to

Oliver than following his astronomer father into the halls of ivy. Why spend your life looking at stars through a telescope when you can be a star yourself?

"You know, Alonee," Sereeta suggested, "maybe this is something that would make Oliver happy. Maybe you should just go along for the ride and share his . . . fun."

"Yeah, right," Alonee whined. "Like I'm a rocker's babe!"

"He's not 'a rocker,' Alonee," Sereeta told her. "He's Oliver, one of the sweetest and most decent guys I've ever met. Other than the dude I'm hanging with, he's just about the most wonderful, caring guy at Tubman. And he loves you, Alonee. Take it from a girlfriend. He loves you."

Alonee sighed deeply. "Thanks, Sereeta. Thanks for keepin' it real."

Then, a moment later, she pointed toward the stage. "Look, they're throwing their stuff at him—their personal stuff. I can't believe it."

Oliver closed his performance with a mashup of Louis Armstrong's "What a Wonderful World" and Radiohead's "No Surprises." Everybody was taking pictures of Oliver before the set ended.

"I just hope he graduates from Tubman," Alonee said grimly.

"Oh, he'll do that," Jaris asserted. "Don't ever think he'd drop out before he got his diploma."

Alonee walked over behind the stage to wait for Oliver.

"Alonee's really bummed out, huh?" Jaris remarked.

"Do you blame her?" Sereeta responded.

"No, but when something like this happens, you gotta go with the flow," Jaris commented. "Alonee cares about Oliver, and she's gotta get behind his dream. Just like years from now, when I win the Nobel Prize in Literature. Babe, I hope you don't say you can't go to Oslo 'cause it's too cold there."

Sereeta gave Jaris a friendly poke in the shoulder. "I'd follow you to Mars, babe," she promised.

Jaris leaned over and kissed Sereeta. He felt so lucky, so blessed to have her. He couldn't imagine life without her.

At school on Monday morning, Jaris was walking from the parking lot. He noticed a young man standing near Harriet Tubman's statue. The guy was looking around and seemed confused, as if lost. He looked nineteen or twenty, maybe younger. But Jaris didn't remember ever seeing him on campus.

"Hi!" Jaris said in a friendly voice. "Can I help you with something?"

"Yeah," the young man replied. "Where're the history classes?"

"Uh, they're spread around in two buildings," Jaris answered. "What class you looking for?"

"There's a Ms. McDowell teaching here, and I want to see her," the man said.

Jaris generally liked people, and he gave them the benefit of the doubt. But some red flags were going up in his mind. He didn't know this guy, who could have all kinds of reasons for wanting to see Ms. McDowell. Maybe he was an old friend of Shane's. Maybe he was older than he looked and was a cop in plainclothes. Jaris felt uncomfortable steering him to Ms. McDowell's classroom. He could just barge in and maybe create a problem.

"Tell you what," Jaris replied "The office is right over there. You see where the two royal palms are? Go to the office and tell them your business. They'll page Ms. McDowell for you."

The man looked unhappy. "Oh, it's okay," he responded. "I didn't think it'd be a big hassle."

"No hassle," Jaris told him. "It's just that anyone coming on campus has to let the office know first. Those are the rules."

"Never mind," the man snarled, turning and hurrying toward the parking lot. He got into a Nissan Altima and drove away, the tires squealing on the blacktop.

"Who was that?" Kevin asked, coming up alongside Jaris.

"Some guy wanting to see Ms. McDowell. When I told him he had to go to the office first, he took off mad," Jaris answered. "That worries me."

"We need to give her a heads-up," Kevin declared.

"Yeah, you're right," Jaris agreed.

The boys walked to Ms. McDowell's classroom, where she was sitting at her desk preparing for the day ahead. She smiled at the boys when they entered the room. You couldn't tell that her heart had to be breaking over her brother and the new trouble he was in. "Good morning," she greeted.

"Ms. McDowell," Jaris said, "I just wanted to let you know something. There was a tall, skinny guy about twenty asking to see you just now. When I told him he needed to check in at the office first, he took off in a Nissan Altima, silver colored."

"Hmmm," Ms. McDowell responded. "Doesn't ring a bell. Well, if it's important, he'll be back. Thanks for telling me."

Kevin and Jaris left Ms. McDowell's classroom and headed for their first classes.

"She's so cool and professional," Kevin remarked. "I don't know how she does it. She must be tore up inside over her brother. I couldn't handle it like that."

"Yeah," Jaris agreed. "I'm with you. If someone I loved was in major trouble like that, I couldn't function."

"That dude was not a cop, Jaris," Kevin commented. "A cop would have done what he needed to do to see Ms. McDowell. Probably would have been smart enough to check in at the office in the first place."

"It's got to have something to do with Shane," Jaris concluded. "I sure hope that kid's troubles don't spill over on Ms. McDowell. Shane probably knows a lotta creepy dudes. Maybe that guy I met was one of them. You know that guy Zendon shot, Buster Bennett? He didn't like the cocaine deal goin' down and called the cops. For that he got offed."

"If I didn't like a drug deal goin' down, I'd just split," Kevin declared. "If I saw dudes trading cocaine for cash, I wouldn't be sending for no ghetto birds. No way. I'd be runnin' away too fast."

"I hear ya, Kev," Jaris agreed. "We're supposed to be good citizens and report stuff like that. But if Buster had just kept his mouth shut and gotten out of there, he'd be playing football this Saturday."

Jaris went on. "Chelsea's friend Sharon saw the whole thing go down. Buster was yelling at his cousin Zendon. Brandon and Shane were, like, right there, waiting for their crack cocaine. Buster went down right in front of them. He was bleeding on the sidewalk. Buster was just a kid, only six-teen. A good kid too. Clean record."

"Yeah," Kevin responded. "A few months before that, his parents were prob-ably goin' in debt to get his teeth straight-ened. They wanted him to have a nice smile.

Then all of a sudden, they're planning their kid's funeral."

"Too many kids going down around here," Jaris lamented. "How many?"

"Rafe Wexford got shot by B.J. Brady," Kevin recalled. "And then Brady went down too. Now Buster."

They walked a few steps in silence, and then Kevin spoke. "I was thinking about Mrs. Jenkins raising four boys in this neighborhood, and they're all good. That woman deserves an award or something. No man to help her. Two boys in the U.S. Army, one in college, and Trevor, our buddy. Probably Mrs. Jenkins worries about her boy over in Afghanistan or somewhere. But if he goes down, at least he died for something. If Mrs. Jenkins loses a boy in the war, people gonna say, 'Another fine young American hero went down to protect our freedom.' "

Kevin looked thoughtful as he continued. "What did Rafe or Buster or B.J. die for? Dudes wanting to use crack cocaine? The homies die, and people say, 'Just another worthless gangbanger outta the way.' "

"Yeah," Jaris agreed. "And the sad part is, Rafe wasn't even a gangbanger. Buster wasn't either."

Oliver joined the boys, looking like his everyday self.

"Hey, man," Kevin asked, "you still hanging out with the common herd, or we gotta consult your agent first?"

Oliver gave Kevin a playful shove. "I got no agent, dude," Oliver responded. "I'm just having fun. It could all end next week, who knows?"

"You're awfully good, Oliver," Jaris remarked. "I'd buy your music."

"I'd download it anyway," Kevin laughed. "You do rock, man."

"You guys see Alonee?" Oliver asked, looking around.

"Yeah, dude. And you better take care of business there," Kevin advised. "That chick needs a big hug and kiss and a lotta sweet talk. She's not so crazy about her man turning into a rock idol."

"Yeah," Oliver admitted sheepishly. "I'm not too popular with Alonee right now."

"Could be," Kevin told him. "Y'know, I think she bought a doll or something at a craft booth on the weekend. Now all she needs is the pins to stick in it."

"Oh, there she is," Oliver said. "Alonee! Wait up!" He hurried over toward Alonee, and in two seconds she was in his arms.

CHAPTER FIVE

Nattie Harvey was the neighborhood gossip. Someone had told her about Brandon Yates and Shane Burgess escaping from the youth detention facility. Although the escape was reported in the newspapers, no names were given because of the boys' ages. Nattie wasted no time in telling everyone she knew, including Jaris's mother.

That night at dinner, Mom brought up the subject. "Those boys are going to be desperate. The police are looking for them, and they have no money, nowhere to stay. I hope Ms. McDowell's being at Tubman won't attract them there. You don't think she'd help them, do you? I mean, that would be abetting criminals. Yet the Burgess boy is her brother."

"Ms. McDowell would never break the law, Mom," Jaris asserted.

"Yes, but she loves that little brother of hers," Mom argued. "How could she refuse him if he showed up scared and hungry."

"She'd make him turn himself in, Mom," Jaris insisted.

"Maybe they just hightailed it up north," Pop suggested.

"Yeah, probably," Jaris agreed to soothe Mom's fears.

"Sharon called me from Grant," Chelsea chimed in. " 'Member, Mom? She was the one that saw Buster get shot. Sharon said some strange guy's been hanging around where Zendon used to live. She never saw him before. He's a tall, skinny guy."

Jaris looked at his little sister. "Chili pepper, did Sharon happen to say the kind of car the guy was driving?"

"No," Chelsea replied. "I'll call her and ask her. She doesn't pay much attention to cars. But Keone, her boyfriend, was with her and he'd probably know. He knows all the cars."

"Yeah, I'd like to know," Jaris told her. Jaris wondered whether the tall, skinny guy who was looking for Ms. McDowell was the same one hanging at Zendon's old apartment.

Chelsea made her phone call, and she had to wait while Sharon talked to Keone. Finally, Chelsea ended the call. "Keone said it was a silver Nissan Altima."

A chill went up Jaris's spine, but he didn't let on to Mom. "Thanks, chili pepper," he said casually. His mother was staring at him as if she sensed he was hiding something.

"Sweetie," Mom asked, "what's that all about? Do you know someone driving that kind of car?"

"No, Mom, I was just curious," Jaris replied, getting up from the table. "I gotta work on my AP American History. We got another evaluation of our projects coming up."

When Jaris got to his laptop, he couldn't work. He was too troubled. That guy at Tubman today had to be the same one hanging around Zendon's old apartment. That meant that whatever was going on had something to do with Shane Burgess. The guy was probably a friend of Shane's. He probably wanted to contact Ms. McDowell on behalf of her brother, who was in hiding. Some creep wanted to put pressure on Ms. McDowell, and that scared Jaris.

At school the next day, Ms. McDowell hailed Jaris. "Do you have a minute?" she asked him.

"Sure, absolutely," Jaris replied. They walked over to a quiet corner of the campus near the science building. Ms. McDowell said, "You and Kevin Walker told me about a young man wanting to see me yesterday. I believe he was driving a Nissan Altima. I think Kevin said that, right?"

"Yeah, that's right," Jaris answered nervously, wondering where she was going.

"Last night when I was in my condo," the teacher explained, "I saw a silver Nissan Altima pass the place twice. I couldn't see who was at the wheel, but I'm sure it was a man. Then he parked across the street."

"Did you call the police?" Jaris asked. "I think you need to—"

"Jaris, I'm sure you know about Shane and Brandon Yates escaping the youth facility," Ms. McDowell interrupted in a sad voice.

"Yeah, Cory Yates told Kevin right after it happened," Jaris told her. "I'm really sorry, Ms. McDowell. I can't tell you how sorry I am."

"I know. Thank you," Ms. McDowell said. "The thing is, I'm not sure if this man in the Nissan has something to do with Shane. He might be trying to get in touch with me to arrange for Shane turning himself in or something."

"The police would stop him and talk to him to find out what he was up to," Jaris suggested.

"Shane got involved with so many strange people while he was on drugs," Ms. McDowell sighed. "But maybe this is a friend, a good kid trying to help him. I don't want to make matters worse. I might just be getting his friend in trouble. And I might lose the chance of contacting Shane and getting him to return to custody."

Ms. McDowell stared thoughtfully at Jaris for a second. "But yes, you're right, Jaris. I need to tell the police what's going on."

"I think so, yeah," Jaris affirmed. "I'm worried about you, Ms. McDowell. I'd feel a lot better if the police were looking out for you."

Ms. McDowell managed a smile. "I haven't had the chance yet to congratulate you for winning second place in that short story contest. That's quite an accomplishment. Mr. Pippin said there were a hundred and twenty entries."

"Thanks," Jaris said. He was touched that Ms. McDowell would remember to congratulate him. She had to be so worried about her little brother. Jaris figured she was really a class act.

That night, Jaris and Kevin arrived at the Chicken Shack at about the same time. They both noticed the Nissan Altima in the parking lot. The tall, skinny guy Jaris had seen at Tubman was getting out of the car. For a terrible moment, Jaris turned numb. What did this guy want? Who was he?

To Jaris's surprise, the guy approached him and Kevin and asked, "Which of you guys is Kevin Walker?"

"I am," Kevin replied. "Who're you, dude?"

"My name's Virgil," the guy answered. "I'm a friend of Cory Yates, and he said you and him know each other."

"Yeah, we know each other," Kevin responded. "Wassup?"

"I loaned Cory's brother, Brandon, and Shane some money a while ago," Virgil explained. "They were restorin' an old car.

We were gonna sell it and share in the profits. Then that thing went down on Grant. Burgess and Yates got busted, and they got sent away owin' me a thousand bucks. I was wondering where those guys might be hiding out now that they busted outta the lockup. If they still got my grand, I'd sure like the money back. Any clue, Kevin?"

Jaris and Kevin exchanged looks. The guy was lying through his teeth with that bull. He wanted to connect with Shane or Brandon—or both—but it had nothing to do with restoring an old car. Maybe they owed him drug money. Or maybe they had hidden a stash when they were all in business together.

"Look, dude," Kevin responded, "the cops are looking for those guys. They're scouring the hood for them. How would I know where they are? I never knew either of them."

"I used to know Shane when he played baseball at Tubman," Jaris added. "But I lost touch with him."

"Shane Burgess has an older sister who teaches at Tubman, right?" Virgil asked. "I was at school the other day lookin' for her, remember? I think I talked to you," he was looking at Jaris. "You think she'd know where him and Yates are?"

Jaris's eyes narrowed, and he spoke sternly. "Dude, let me be real clear. She doesn't know where her brother is. She has no idea. If you got any brains, you'll keep real far away from her and not be driving in front of her condo. Y'hear what I'm saying? She's already told the cops about you doing that, so don't be doing it anymore."

Jaris had his attention and continued. "I don't know what you want with Shane Burgess, but I'm not buying the crap about old cars, man. Shane's sister wants her brother back in custody so he can straighten out. If he shows up near her, she'd call the cops. But he knows that, and he would never put her on the spot. If you hassle her again, man, you're gonna be picked up."

Virgil was silent for a moment. Then he responded. "I just wanna talk to the lady. The neighbors said her brother lived there at the condo pretty recently. I get what you're sayin', man, and I won't bother the lady. I'm cool."

"Good," Jaris said.

Virgil turned and walked back to his Altima. Before he got in, he turned and glanced at Kevin and Jaris. They were still standing in the parking lot outside the Chicken Shack. Then he drove off.

"Man," Jaris asked, "waddya make of that, Kevin?"

"The guy doesn't seem like a gangbanger or a dopehead," Kevin remarked. "But he's got a real need to meet up with Shane and Brandon for some reason. I believe you convinced him to leave Ms. McDowell alone, though."

Before he and Kevin went in to start their shift, Jaris got on his cell phone and called Torie McDowell. He ran the name

"Virgil" past her. He told her what the guy had said.

"That name doesn't ring a bell," Ms. McDowell replied.

"He wants to connect with Brandon and Shane real bad," Jaris told her. "And he was shadowing you, thinking you might know where they are. I told him you don't know, and if you found out, you'd tell the cops. I told him to stay away from Tubman and your condo. If he doesn't, he'll be picked up by the cops 'cause they know about him. He seemed to buy that."

"Thanks, Jaris," Ms. McDowell responded. "Thank you so much."

Jaris and Kevin went into the Chicken Shack then and donned their work shirts.

Jaris worked alongside Amberlynn Parson for most of the evening. As usual, she was very efficient. Jaris marveled at how cool she remained even when the lines were long and some of the customers got impatient. She calmed them down with that amazing smile of hers.

About an hour before quitting time, the door opened and Virgil reappeared. He ignored Kevin and Jaris and ordered a crispy chicken wrap in Amberlynn's line. "I'll have a strawberry smoothie too," he added.

"How's the rag business, Virgil?" Amberlynn asked. Virgil was at the end of the line, and no more customers were waiting for service. A few were eating in the booths.

"Pretty dull, Amberlynn," Virgil answered. "Not too many guys buying new suits. They're making do with their old ones, but we're selling shirts and ties."

Both Kevin and Jaris stared at Virgil and Amberlynn who were talking like old friends. Amberlynn was smiling at the young man. He took his crispy chicken wrap and smoothie in a bag and headed for the door. He glanced back at Amberlynn and said, "Take it easy, girl." Then he was gone. The silver Nissan Altima disappeared into the night. Virgil had never even looked at Kevin and Jaris.

"You *know* that dude?" Jaris asked Amberlynn.

"Yeah, why?" the girl answered. "He used to go to Lincoln. He played basketball. He was a senior when I was a freshman. I was a cheerleader, and we got to know each other that way. He's a real nice guy. He works in the men's clothing store over by Lincoln."

Kevin was standing nearby. "You know the guy well?" he asked.

"We were friends," Amberlynn shrugged. "But when he graduated, we kinda lost touch. I haven't seen him in maybe a year and a half until just now. You know how it is. When guys graduate, they don't always keep up with the kids still stuck in school. I think his name is Dunne or Dunston, something like that. I didn't know his family or anything."

Jaris and Kevin were both trying to get the connection between this ordinary young guy and Brandon and Shane. Kevin was more willing than Jaris to be blunt.

"Amberlynn, is this Virgil dude into drugs or anything, do you know?"

"I don't think so," she replied. "He sure wasn't when he played basketball. Coach wouldn't even let the guys smoke. I don't think he even drank. From what I saw, he seemed like a straight arrow."

"Lotta dudes messing with drugs around here," Kevin remarked. Kevin and Jaris thought Virgil's need to find Brandon and Shane *had* to have something to do with drugs. Virgil maybe sold them some junk and never got paid. Or maybe he paid for some junk and never got it. Amberlynn believed Virgil was so clean and pure, but Kevin figured she was naïve.

The next day, Oliver came down to eat with the gang under the eucalyptus trees, but Alonee wasn't with him. "She had to go to the library," Oliver explained.

"How's it goin' with you two?" Sami asked. "Seem to me like she ticked off every time I see her, and that's not like my girlfriend."

"We're fine," Oliver asserted.

"Yeah?" Sami asked. "She don't act like she's fine, dude. I don't think she ever figured on a rock 'n' roll idol for her man."

Oliver laughed. "I'm far from that. I'm just helping out my old friends."

"Come on, dude," Kevin remarked. "You're lovin' every minute of this ride. Nothin' to be ashamed of, man. We all wanna live some fabulous life that's fun and exciting—and with lots of money maybe. If I were you, I'd ride this roller coaster as far as it takes me. You'd be a freakin' fool not to."

"Oh, I'm not going to con myself into thinking this is going to amount to much," Oliver insisted.

"You still planning to go to college after we graduate from Tubman?" Jaris asked.

"Uh, yeah, I guess so," Oliver replied. "Eventually—"

"Eventually?" Sami asked. "What's that mean, boy?"

"Some dude contacted me," Oliver started to explain. "He came to the house and said he wanted me to do a demo. I don't think anything'll come of it. He just asked if I was interested, and I said sure, why not? I imagine a million demos are done every year and don't go anywhere."

"Just some dude off the street," Kevin asked, "or somebody with cred?"

Oliver answered slowly. "Well, my father talked to him, and he kinda looked into it. Seems like this guy has some pretty big names in his stable, not that I'm under any illusions that I could join them."

"Wow!" Sami cried. "Next year this time, you prob'ly won't even be wantin' to talk to us, man. We'll have to get in line to see you, like groupies."

"You'll always be my friends," Oliver stated solemnly, with a smirk on his face. "Even when I'm rich and famous. I'll invite you to my palatial home in Malibu. And then I'll give you all rides in my Rolls Royce. You can come to my concerts free.

Any member of Alonee's posse is always welcome in my inner circle."

Oliver started laughing as he spoke. He quickly added, "I'm just a little frog in a big pond. If I cut a record, maybe two hundred people'll buy it. But I gotta admit, right now I'm having fun. I'll always remember this when I'm a boring old college teacher putting my students to sleep." Oliver made his voice sound creaky, like an old man's. "I'll tell my students, 'Once I was cool. I wasn't always a long-winded old fossil.' "

Suddenly the smile left Oliver's face, and he turned serious and a little sad. "You guys, help me with Alonee. Try to help her see it can be fun for her too. I haven't morphed into some strange freak. I want her to enjoy this too."

"But, dude," Kevin protested, "you *have* morphed into some strange freak. When I see you singing on the stage, I don't recognize you."

"I can't imagine what's wrong with that girl," Sami declared. "She used to love this nice, normal dude. Now he's turned into a wild rock 'n' roller with all kinds of strange girls screamin' at him and droolin' and stuff. Don' know why, but Alonee don't like that. What's *wrong* with the girl? What chick wouldn't be thrilled to pieces to have her boyfriend the dreamboat for a zillion other chicks? I know if Matson Malloy got to be a rock idol, I'd ditch him in a blink."

"You're a big help, Sami," Oliver groaned.

Alonee appeared then at the top of the trail, walking down slowly. She carried her brown bag with salad and a homemade chicken wrap. She looked at Oliver, a smile flickering on her lips, and spoke to him.

"You know, Oliver, I've been thinking," she told him. "Maybe Marko was right, and we were all wrong. He said you were an alien from outer space. Maybe Oliver Randall is an illusion, and you really are Antar from a distant star."

Oliver covered his face with his hands and moaned.

CHAPTER SIX

Chelsea didn't get too many chances to see her friend Sharon, who lived over on Grant Street. So on Saturday, Jaris drove Chelsea and Athena over there. They picked up Sharon and her friend, Keone Lowe, and headed for the mall.

"How's everything on Grant?" Jaris asked Sharon and Keone.

"It's a nasty and noisy at night," Sharon answered. "None of us can sleep. They're yellin' an' fightin' an' drinkin' an' smashin' their bottles in the street."

"Gangbangers standin' around all the time," Keone added. "And you better not look at 'em, man. You just look at 'em, and you in big trouble. I just look down at the ground when I'm near them."

"Maybe you guys can move away from there pretty soon," Chelsea said. "That would be so cool."

"I don't know," Sharon sighed. "Ma said we're getting help with the rent where we live, and we wouldn't get that just any-where. I just wish the ones making the trou-ble would move away."

"Zendon, he was a bad character, and now he's gone, in jail," Athena said. "Didn't that help?"

"No," Keone replied. "Some other guys come in an' take over his business. Dealin' goin' on as bad as before. They like rats, those drug dealers. They multiply fast."

"Do you recognize the guys dealing?" Jaris asked.

Sharon and Keone looked at one an-other with fear in their eyes. "Sometime we know 'em," Keone responded. "But we don't mess with 'em."

"My mama," Sharon explained with a shudder, "she come out one night. She yelled at them. She told them they got no business selling crack cocaine where young kids playing on their skateboards. They just laugh at her and go, 'Hey, old lady, you like a bomb comin' in your window some night?' "

Jaris shook his head. "What about the cops? Don't they do anything?"

"Yeah, sometime they come around," Keone answered. "Ghetto bird shines the big lights down on them. But the drug dealers like cockroaches. You shine a light, and they run and hide. Soon's it's dark again, they come out, same as before."

"You guys know Cory Yates? He drives a silver Mercedes," Jaris asked. "Is he one of the dealers?"

There was dead silence in the car. Jaris looked in the rearview mirror at Sharon and Keone. "Sharon, you know who he is, don't you?"

"His brother and some other dude dealin'," Sharon replied in a small voice. "I don't mess with 'em, though."

Jaris felt cold. Had Brandon Yates and Shane Burgess taken over Zendon's territory? The thought of it made him sick to his stomach.

They went onto the freeway and soon turned into the parking structure for the mall. The world was different here, bright and clean and happy, far from the dirt and evil on Grant. Sharon, Keone, Chelsea, and Athena jumped from the Ford Focus. The stores were running big sales today, especially at Lawson's. The girls were clutching their coupons.

Inside Lawson's, Keone wasn't interested in much beyond shoes. He needed shoes. He loved sports, but his shoes were worn out. Jaris left the three girls in the teen fashion section, and he and Keone went to the shoe department.

"I ain't got much money," Keone confided. "Pa just give me a twenty, so I'll mainly just be lookin', Jaris. Later on, when I can put more money to the twenty, I'll get me a pair."

"What do you play, Keone?" Jaris asked.

"Basketball, man. I love basketball," Keone answered, with passion in his voice. "I like Shaq and Kobe and stuff." Keone's pace quickened as they neared a display of shoes with swooshes on them.

"I'm gonna be a big basketball star when I grow up," Keone declared, a smile breaking out on his face. "I'm gonna get a big house for Ma and Pa, so far away from Grant, I'm gonna forget we ever been there."

Keone took a pair of athletic shoes off the display and cradled them tenderly in his hands. "These here're my size. I'll get them sometime when I got more money. These are the best. They cost more 'n double the money I got."

Jaris had put three hundred of his five-hundred-dollar prize money in his savings account. He'd kept two hundred out in cash, and it was now in his wallet. He took the shoes from Keone and asked, "These are what you need, eh?"

"Yeah, man, but I only got twenty," Keone replied.

"Maybe they're on sale. Everything's supposed to be on sale," Jaris suggested. When they got to the cash register, they learned that the shoes were marked down ten dollars. But they still cost forty dollars. "With discount, you can get these, Keone," Jaris told the boy.

"For real?" Keone cried, his face lighting up and his eyes getting big. "I can get them *now*?"

Jaris took the boy's twenty dollar bill and gave him back five singles in change. He paid the rest from his cash. The clerk handed Keone the box, and he hugged it as if it were a treasure. "You sure I still get change?" he asked.

"Uh-huh," Jaris answered. "Let's go see what the girls are up to, Keone. We don't wanna leave them alone too long. They're probably getting into all kinds of mischief, buying out the store."

Keone laughed.

Chelsea and Athena were running from rack to rack, but Sharon held back, intimidated by all the clothes. She was standing near some plaid tops that just came in.

"You like them, Sharon?" Jaris asked.

"Yeah, I like the plaids. Some girls at school have them, but they cost a lot," Sharon answered.

"No, look," Jaris pointed out. "They're on sale. You can get three of them for the price of one."

"My ma only give me ten dollars," Sharon said, pulling five ones and a crinkled five from her purse.

"That'll do it, Sharon," Jaris told her. "Pick out three in your size that you like."

"But it says they cost fifteen dollars each," Sharon objected. "So even if you can get three for one, it's still fifteen dollars."

"No, I got some coupons here," Jaris fibbed. "Just pick three of them out, honey."

Sharon picked out a red and white plaid, a green and white, and a striking yellow and black. "You sure, Jaris? You sure I can afford all these?"

Jaris smiled and assured her, "Yep." He glanced across the floor to see Athena staggering under a huge load of clothing. He figured her parents didn't spend a lot of time with her. So they made up by giving her all the money she needed.

Athena spent almost two hundred dollars. Chelsea wanted to spend seventy-five until Jaris made her put back two tops with plunging necklines.

"You get three bucks back in change, Sharon," Jaris said.

Sharon didn't say anything, but she gave Jaris a big hug. Jaris had pulled a fast one on Keone, but Sharon knew what he had done.

The five of them headed for the food court.

"I am gonna look so awesome in my new stuff," Athena remarked, carrying three large bags.

They all ordered hot dogs and sodas, and then they stopped again for ice cream. Athena treated everybody to all the food. Jaris had to admit that, for all the girl's faults, she did have a generous heart.

When they got back to Grant, Jaris got out of the car to make sure Keone and Sharon got into their building safely. Sharon gave Jaris another hug and went inside. Keone shook his hand. "Thanks, dude, for everything." Then Keone said, "Man, can we talk?"

"Sure, Keone," Jaris responded. Jaris and Keone walked under a mulberry tree with big, yellowing leaves. It was one of the few pretty things on Grant.

"Dude, I'm not tellin' you this, okay?" Keone whispered.

"Deal," Jaris agreed.

"The ones dealing crack cocaine are the guys with Zendon the night Buster Bennett was taken down," Keone said softly. "They been gone for a while. Now they back."

A wave of nausea swept over Jaris. It was what he suspected. Shane and Brandon.

Sharon dropped hints, but now Keone confirmed that they were around.

"Remember," Keone insisted, "I never told you."

"You got it, man," Jaris assured him.

Jaris drove Athena home and dropped Chelsea off at the house. Then he drove to Kevin's grandparents' house. Kevin had said he was going to help his grandparents plant some trees today. When Jaris pulled into the driveway, Kevin was digging a hole in the front yard. A pot containing a bright green tree sat there, waiting to be planted.

"Orange tree?" Jaris asked.

"Yeah," Kevin replied. "Grandpa said he'll never live to see the oranges, but it's for my kids."

"Kevin," Jaris began, "I found out something pretty awful, and I don't know what to do with it."

Kevin dropped the shovel and waited. "Lay it on me, dude," he said.

"Shane and Brandon, they're dealing over on Grant," Jaris told him. "They were before they got busted, and now they're back at it."

Kevin closed his eyes for a second and shook his head. "Oh man! Oh man! It doesn't get any worse than that," he groaned.

"Yeah," Jaris agreed.

The two boys sat on an overturned log in the front yard of the Stevens's farm. Jaris remembered what Ms. McDowell had told them: her had parents died of drug overdoses, and she alone was able to salvage her life. She lost three siblings to crack cocaine, and she was desperately trying to save her younger brother.

"Kevin, what do I do now?" Jaris asked.

"Man, what *can* you do?" Kevin asked. "The cops know what's going on down there. They're hanging there three to four times a week. The ghetto birds are like vultures on a carcass. One o' these nights, they'll get Shane and Brandon. You can't make it happen, and you can't stop it from happening."

"Do I tell Ms. McDowell?" Jaris asked.

"Jaris, you didn't see this going down with your own eyes, right?" Kevin reasoned. "You got it secondhand? It's probably true, but you're not one hundred percent sure if you didn't see it happening. Don't hit her with this. She has to be guessing the worst anyway. Maybe that lady is just hanging onto a thread of hope. Don't take that away from her, y'hear what I'm sayin'?"

"Yeah, thanks, man," Jaris said, shaking Kevin's hand. "Good luck with the orange tree, and say hi to your grandparents for me."

At Spain's Auto Repair, the installers were putting in the new smog equipment. Pop was standing there, smiling. "Ah, this is gonna be great, Jaris," he declared as his son came walking up. Pop was brimming with optimism. He threw an arm around Jaris's shoulders "I been telling everybody about you winning that big prize in the story contest, Jaris. You made me so proud. You always make me so proud. If I never done anything in my life but raise you two great kids, I guess I'd be a big success, huh?"

Pop's happy smile faded then as he noticed the expression on Jaris's face. "Wassup, boy? Somethin' wrong?" he asked.

Jaris took a long, deep breath before answering. "Pop, Shane Burgess and Brandon Yates are dealing drugs over around Grant. They busted out of jail, and now they're pushing crack cocaine."

Pop whistled. "We knew the punks were on the loose, but to be doin' that . . . Oh brother, your poor teacher! That wonderful lady!"

"I wish there was something I could do, Pop," Jaris said.

"I know," Pop told him. "Lissen, I know this cop, he's a good friend, and he's a cool guy. I'll give him a heads-up for whatever it's worth. It'd be good if the punks could be caught. Who knows, maybe more time in the slammer would straighten them out."

"Pop, this is, like, ruining Ms. McDowell's life," Jaris groaned. "Y'know what I'm saying? She'd probably like to get married and start a family, but how can she with this hanging over her head? She's a beautiful, wonderful lady, and she doesn't deserve this. It's just not fair." Jaris's voice was filled with anguish.

"Boy," Pop declared, "life ain't fair. Ain't you figured that one out yet? You do the best you can, but life keeps throwing you curveballs. The cops'll get the punks. We can only hope they get a chance to make a decent life somewhere down the road."

Jaris felt so disturbed that night, he didn't want to stay home. He wasn't scheduled to work at the Chicken Shack. He'd planned to work on his AP American History class work, but he couldn't. He needed to get his mind off things.

Kevin was busy with Carissa, and Trevor had gone somewhere with Denique. Sereeta was taking her grandmother to a play she had been wanting to see for a long time. Sereeta's grandma, Bessie Prince, didn't eat out much, and this was a special gift from Sereeta. They'd attend the play and then go to dinner.

Jaris punched in Oliver Randall's number. He might be rehearsing with Life of Amphibians, getting ready to be Antar again this weekend. Or maybe he was arranging his dreadlocks or picking out a new vest. But it was worth a try.

"Oliver, you busy?" Jaris asked.

"Hey, Jaris," Oliver replied. "Me and my dad are sitting here discussing the national debt and how my kids and grandkids are gonna pay for it. Pop's nodding off, and I'm bored out of my gourd. What's up, Jare?"

"I'm so bummed out, Oliver. I need a friend," Jaris confided.

"Hang tight, dude," Oliver ordered. "I'm giving Pop permission to go to bed, and I'm hopping in the BMW. I'll be there in ten minutes."

"You're not in dreadlocks, are you?" Jaris asked.

"No, and no rhinestone vest either," Oliver replied.

Oliver was at Jaris's home in twelve minutes. Jaris jumped in the car with him, and soon they were going up a winding road into the hills.

"So, my friend," Oliver asked, "what's got you so bummed?"

"Oh man!" Jaris groaned. "I found out that Ms. McDowell's brother and this other dude have been selling crack cocaine over on Grant. They been doing this since they busted out of jail. I feel so bad for Ms. McDowell. She's tried so hard to save her brother, and this is gonna be bad."

"I'm really sorry to hear that, Jaris," Oliver said. "I guess it's awfully hard to kick drugs, and Shane must be in pretty deep. When you need the stuff so bad yourself, you gotta turn to selling to pay for your own habit."

"My pop knows a cop who deals with gangs and drugs," Jaris added. "He's letting him know what's happening. I hope they catch Shane and Brandon before something worse happens."

Jaris looked around and asked, "Where we going?"

"You'll see," Oliver said.

Oliver slowed down as they approached a small, round building high in the mountains.

"What's that?" Jaris asked.

"My dad's friend Sam Bailey, he and his wife live up here sometimes and they do research on the skies," Oliver explained. "They have this observatory. They got telescopes way better than the amateurs in the park, Jaris."

When they got out of the car, both boys looked down into the valley below. It was an unbelievable sight. The city had so many lights that it looked like a jewelry box.

"That's awesome," Jaris remarked. "I've never seen the whole city from a spot like this. I should bring Sereeta here. She'd love it."

"Anytime, dude," Oliver said. "Talk about a romantic spot, huh? I'm gonna talk Alonee into coming up here with me. I figure that'll make her forget Antar."

They went into the observatory, and Oliver introduced Jaris to the Baileys. They opened the ceiling, and Jaris looked through the telescope.

"The moon! Oh my gosh! It's like right in my face," Jaris gasped. "I see the mountains of the moon. They're so clear, so close. It's like the moon is in the backyard . . ."

"When I'm really confused and I need to get away from everything, I come up here," Oliver explained. "I look up into the sky, and—I don't know—it helps. It makes me calm."

Oliver refocused the telescope and beckoned to Jaris to come look. Jaris peered through the lens, and suddenly there was Saturn, rings and all.

"Wow!" Jaris whispered. "There they are, just like in my story—'Rings of Saturn.' Man, Oliver, seeing Saturn so close, it's, like, awesome."

When they finished looking at the sky, Mr. and Mrs. Bailey served them ginger ale and lacy sugar cookies. They all sat talking for a while. During their conversation, Jaris watched the incredible sky, with the moon and shining planets and stars. He then looked at the city sparkling below in the valley. It all seemed so far away from the ugliness of Grant and the terrible problems there.

Yet even here, Jaris could not completely forget Shane Burgess. Jaris's memory traveled back to the bright day on the baseball diamond at Tubman High School. Shane—the guy they all called "Sparky"—had pitched a big win. Jaris could still hear the cheers of the crowd and see the happy young man jogging off the field. He seemed on his way. He was fresh-faced and healthy. It didn't seem possible that he would be thrown in prison, escape, and deal drugs.

On the drive home, Jaris made a comment to Oliver. "I bet Ms. McDowell is sitting in her condo right now crying, man."

114

"Yeah," Oliver agreed. "My heart goes out to her."

As they drew near the Spains' home, Jaris asked, "So, Oliver, do you imagine yourself being a scientist or a rocker?"

"Both!" Oliver answered promptly. "Both!"

CHAPTER SEVEN

On Friday night at ten o'clock, Chelsea got a call from her friend Sharon on Grant. It was late for anybody to be calling Chelsea, so she grabbed her phone nervously.

"Chelsea," Sandra gasped breathlessly. "They're shootin' up the street. It's awful. We're so scared. We're all hidin' in the apartment. We're afraid to go near the window. It's like pop-pop-pop!"

"Are the cops there?" Chelsea asked.

"They're comin'. We hear the sirens. The helicopter too. Oh, Chelsea, this is worse than anything that ever happened here!" Sandra was crying. "Keone and his family's hidin' too."

"It'll be okay when the cops get there," Chelsea assured her friend. "Don't go near the doors or windows. Call me back when it's over, Sharon. Call me back right away!"

Mom and Pop heard Chelsea talking on the phone, and they came into her room. "What's hap'nin'?" Pop asked.

"Oh, Sharon just called from Grant!" Chelsea cried. "There's shooting going on real bad. Somebody shooting up the street, and Sharon and her mom are so scared. I guess the gangs are fighting or something. Sharon's whole family is like down on the floor 'cause they're afraid the bullets will come in the windows."

Pop's eyes narrowed. "It ain't right," he fumed, anger filling his eyes. "It ain't right that they should be terrorized by the punks. This is America. It's right there in the Constitution. We're entitled to life, liberty, and the pursuit of happiness. What kind of happiness they got over there on Grant with stuff like that goin' on?"

Jaris had come into the hallway and listened. His thoughts went immediately to Shane and Brandon. Were they over on Grant tonight? Were they mixed up in this? Jaris went into the living room and turned on the TV news. The broadcast was live, a report on the violence.

The Spains gathered in the living room, staring at the TV screen. Police cars were everywhere on the scene.

"Everything is pretty sketchy at this point," the on-scene reporter said in a terse voice. "The neighbors are saying there was an execution-style shooting. I'm looking over to the corner of Grant and Skyview right now, and I can see at least two people down. A witness said a car came speeding in front of the apartments and shots were fired from the car. The car then sped away, but the police took a young man into custody about a mile from the scene. We don't know at this time if he was the shooter."

Chelsea's phone rang. "Yeah?" she said anxiously.

"Chelsea," Sharon said, "the cops are all over. We're so glad to see them. I wish they'd stay here all the time. We're okay. Keone called me, and he's okay too. I think some guys got killed, Chelsea. I'm looking out my window, and they're putting covers over some people . . . on the sidewalk. I think they're, you know, dead."

When Chelsea hung up, she told her parents and Jaris what Sharon had said. "Sharon and Keone and their families are okay, but somebody's dead—maybe two people."

"Somebody's child," Mom sighed in a deeply sad voice. "Some boy's parents struggling to raise a son, and now he's dead. They probably fed him vitamins and worried about his teeth. God in heaven, when did all this start? Children killing children? How did we get here? How did we lose our way so bad?"

Pop put his arm around Mom's shoulders. "I hear ya, babe," he consoled her. "It's enough to tear your heart out. You see these little kids on the street maybe taggin', doin' vandalism. Then pretty soon they're in the big time—crack, gangs, guns. You can see them slippin' away little by little."

The news report remained live for the next thirty minutes. No names of the dead were given, pending notification of next of kin. A young man had been arrested, but his name was also withheld. The coroner was on the scene, and the news anchor closed her report somberly.

"Two young men, probably teenagers, are dead," she reported, "and the police have a suspect in custody. We'll bring you updates as this sad story unfolds."

Jaris went to bed, but he couldn't sleep. When something like this happened, he always wondered who died. Was a friend caught up in the shooting? Did Kevin Walker stop to see what was going on and get shot? Did Trevor Jenkins get caught in the cross-fire on his way home? Jaris dreaded the thought of his cell phone ringing and hearing terrible news. Kevin's grandparents?

Trevor's mom? But the phone didn't ring, and the dawn came up red.

Saturday was a new day, and Jaris worked tonight at the Chicken Shack. He was planning to chill with Sereeta in the early afternoon, maybe grab some hot dogs. It would be a routine day. Maybe the names of the dead would be given. If so and if Jaris didn't know them, he'd feel momentarily sad but then let it go. He figured guys on the battlefield must go through this. You hoped nobody in your unit went down, and you were sorry that anybody went down. But if your friends made it out okay, you breathed a sigh of relief.

As the Spains were finishing breakfast, Kevin Walker came over on his motorcycle. Jaris went out to the front yard to talk to him. Kevin looked terrible. The sight of him turned Jaris numb even before a word was spoken.

"I talked to Cory Yates," Kevin reported. "Brandon's dead. He was one of the guys shot on Grant last night."

121

Jaris stared wordlessly at Kevin, who looked grief stricken. He wasn't that close to Cory and certainly not to Brandon. So why did Kevin look bad? Jaris's heart raced. He thought he knew the reason. He didn't want to hear the words confirming it, though. As long as Kevin didn't say the dreaded words, it wasn't so.

Brandon and Shane were together when they busted out of jail. They were together selling crack cocaine. Were they together last night?

"Kevin," Jaris finally forced the words out, "was Shane—?"

"He's gone too, Jaris," Kevin replied.

Jaris and Kevin went into the house and told Jaris's parents and Chelsea. Kevin sank down on the sofa, his face in his hands. Jaris sat beside him, his arm around his shoulders.

"Poor Ms. McDowell," Jaris finally sighed. He felt near tears. He could imagine her sorrow.

"I'm so sorry, sweetheart," Mom consoled him. "What a terrible tragedy."

Pop just stood there in stunned silence. Then he announced, "Monie, we gotta go see her."

"We will when she gets—" Mom started to say.

"Now," Pop insisted. "We'll all go over there as a family. Chelsea, you wanna go, right, little girl?"

"Yes," Chelsea responded. She had seen the teacher around Tubman many times, though Ms. McDowell didn't teach any freshman classes. Jaris had talked a lot about her junior and senior history courses, and Chelsea was looking forward to being in her classes.

"We'll stop by Sereeta's place and see if she wants to come too," Pop commanded.

Jaris called Sereeta. He told her what happened, and she began to cry. Yes, she wanted to come with the Spain family to see Ms. McDowell.

The Spains pulled up to Torie McDowell's condominium. Other cars were there already. Jaris recognized the Archers' van and the Lennoxes' car. When the Spains and Sereeta walked in, Ms. McDowell was sitting on her couch with Mattie Archer beside her. Mom went over and gave Ms. McDowell a hug.

Mattie's rich, soothing voice filled the room. "Darlin', the boy is with the Lord now. The Lord has mercy on his wayward children. He gonna be safe now. No more gangs, no more drugs. He in the arms of the Lord. He home."

Torie McDowell looked as though she had been crying, but she was composed now. She was visibly brokenhearted, but she spoke warmly and gratefully to all her students and friends. She thanked them for coming and said their visit meant a lot to her. As the Spains were leaving, Pastor Bromley and his wife, Viola, were coming in. They both took Ms. McDowell in their arms.

"Lotta people love that woman," Pop remarked as they got into Jaris's car. "That funeral, everybody gonna be there. That little Holiness Awakenin' Church gonna be full to the brim, full of love for her. She's gonna be all right."

Jaris took his family home, and then took Sereeta to a little coffee shop. They found a booth far in the back and had just coffee. "I thought she'd succeed with him," Sereeta said forlornly. "I really did."

Jaris took a deep shuddering breath.

"Nobody coulda tried harder," she went on. "She did her best. Lotta people criticized her when she took Shane into her condo, but she stuck with him. She loved him with all her heart." Sereeta shook her head. "It all seems so futile sometimes," she commented. "It all seems hopeless."

"But you gotta keep on trying, Sereeta," Jaris insisted. "You gotta pick yourself up and go on and keep on trying to make a difference. You mark my words. Ms. McDowell is gonna be okay. Things'll never be the same for her, but she'll keep on giving her all for the kids. She's bent, but she's not broken."

"I wonder what happened last night," Sereeta said. "I heard on the news this morning that it wasn't a gang fight. A car just drove up, and the guy opened fire. It was like an execution. Brandon and Shane were just shot down, and then the guy sped away. The cops caught up to him real quick, and he didn't put up a fight. The news guy said he surrendered quick. It was like he knew he wouldn't get away, but he had to give it a shot."

When Jaris and Sereeta were back in the car, Jaris turned on the radio. In a few minutes, the local news came on.

Two teenagers died in a shooting last night at Grant and Skyview. Police are charging a nineteen-year-old man with the shootings. The names of the dead are not yet being released, but the police have in custody Virgil Dunston, formerly a student at Lincoln High School.

"Virgil Dunston!" Jaris cried. "That's the guy who was trying to talk to Ms. McDowell. He wanted to get in touch with Brandon and Shane."

"Isn't that the guy you said Amberlynn knew?" Sereeta asked. "You said he came in the Chicken Shack, and she was talking to him."

"Yeah," Jaris answered. "She said he was a nice guy. No drugs or anything. Wow! He was looking for those boys to kill them!"

"But why?" Sereeta asked.

Jaris took Sereeta home, and then he went home himself. When he got to his room, he punched in Amberlynn's phone number.

"Amberlynn, you heard?" Jaris began.

"Oh, Jaris!" she gasped. "It just came over the radio that Virgil Dunston killed those two guys. I was so shocked. I talked to my parents about it, and they said his half brother was Buster Bennett. That was the kid who was killed on Grant a few months ago. I never knew that, Jaris. Pop said the guys had different fathers, but they were raised together by their mom. Pop said Virgil really loved his little brother. Pop knows Virgil's father 'cause they belong to the same lodge. He said Virgil went to pieces when he lost his brother."

"But Zendon Corman killed his brother," Jaris said. "He's in jail now, waiting for his trial."

"My father said Virgil blamed Shane and Brandon too," Amberlynn explained. "He thought they were all in the crack cocaine business together. That's why Buster got killed, 'cause he was going to blow the lid off the whole thing."

"Oh man!" Jaris groaned.

"I guess as long as Brandon and Shane were in that youth prison, Virgil kinda let it go," Amberlynn suggested. "But when they busted out and were back on the street dealing crack, he just went kinda crazy. It's so sad, Jaris. Virgil isn't a bad guy. He was always nice to me. He was always a gentleman. But those guys, they wasted his brother, and now they were starting up again. I guess he just lost it."

"Lotta families grieving today, Amberlynn," Jaris remarked sadly before he ended the conversation.

Jaris felt sick all day. He tried to go about his usual routine. He helped Pop plant some rose bushes in the front yard. Mom loved rose bushes. She had been wanting more in the front yard for a long time, but Pop kept putting it off.

"Never liked rose bushes," Pop commented. "Too many thorns. Like life, eh, Jare?"

"I hear ya," Jaris responded. He told his father about Virgil Dunston being Buster Bennett's brother. "It was a vengeance killing, Pop. Virgil figured Shane and Brandon had to know Zendon was gonna off his brother. Virgil figured they were all in it together. That's the way around here. Somebody goes down, and his friends take somebody else down. It's a vicious cycle."

"Well, one more to go," Pop remarked. He was ready to dig the hole for the last rose bush.

"I wonder what the Yates family is feelin' like?" Pop mused as he pushed the spade into the soft earth. "They never would rein those boys in. Cory, Brandon, both runnin' wild. The parents just let it happen. It's the parents, Jaris. That's where the blame is. Poor Torie McDowell, she did all she could for her brother. But the parents, they dropped the ball a long time ago. They were dopers, and their kids were dopers. Nothin' short of a miracle that Ms. McDowell rose above all that and made a beautiful life, but the kid couldn't."

Pop was shoveling dirt quickly, pushing the spade into the hole harder and harder. "Shane," he went on, "he just couldn't rise above that stuff. I'm tellin' ya, boy, ain't no job on the Lord's green earth as important as being a good parent. You get your babies when the clay is nice and soft, and you get the chance to mold 'em. Y'hear what

I'm sayin'? You gotta give 'em love, and you gotta give 'em discipline. You gotta be there for them. You gotta be willin' to have them mad at you for cracking down when you need to."

Pop was finally content with the size of the hole. He laid the shovel aside. Jaris placed the bush in the hole and poured water around the roots.

"Jaris," Pop declared as his son finished up, "I don't care what nobody says. Bein' a parent, that's the most important job in this here world. You flunk there, and you ruined lives for good."

Pop stepped back and swiveled his gaze along the line of freshly planted bushes. "There. She oughta like that," he commented. "She's gonna have pink and red roses all over the place. She says she wants everybody comin' up the driveway to see them. Look okay, boy?"

"Looks perfect, Pop," Jaris replied. "You know what?"

"What's that, Jaris?"

"You didn't flunk. You made an A," Jaris told his father.

For a minute, Pop didn't say anything. Then he smiled. "Ya think?" he asked.

"I *know*," Jaris affirmed.

The funeral for Shane Burgess was held on Wednesday afternoon after school. That way, students who wanted to attend could do so without missing classes. The Holiness Awakening Church was filled with more flowers than Jaris had ever seen before for a funeral.

The whole Spain family came along with the Lennoxes and the Archers. Kevin Walker came with his grandparents, and many students from Ms. McDowell's classes at Tubman showed up. Some had taken her classes five or six years ago, and they came with spouses and babies and toddlers. Mr. Pippin and Mr. Myers and all the teachers from Tubman came. Ms. McDowell sat in the first pew with Mr. Pippin, Jaris and Sereeta, Oliver and Alonee, Sami and her family. Because Ms. McDowell had no living relatives, the students who loved her in a special way sat near her. Sereeta sat right next to Ms. McDowell, and throughout the ceremony, their hands were clasped together. From that day in the past when Ms. McDowell had talked Sereeta out of her darkest mood, the teacher had become Sereeta's big sister forever.

Pastor Bromley gave a beautiful homily on the mercy of God. He talked about Shane's triumphs on the baseball field. He described how the boy had just last year raised money for breast cancer research. He said that the boy had a difficult time in his youth and that, sadly, in the end he was not strong enough to heal his brokenness.

"God, who is love, understands this," Pastor Bromley intoned. "He made us. He knows we try, but often we fail. We judge one another, and we shouldn't. Only God sees our hearts. Now Shane Burgess has gone into the light, into the loving arms of his Maker, just a boy, a troubled boy, but still a child of God."

Jaris had never heard Pastor Bromley so eloquent. Torie McDowell was softly weeping.

Blue and golden flowers lay atop the casket in honor of the Tubman baseball team, on which Shane had played. A folded jersey lay on the casket, and a golden ribbon read, "Good-bye, Sparky."

The casket was carried from Holiness Awakening Church by pallbearers chosen by Ms. McDowell. They were Mr. Pippin, Jaris, Oliver, Trevor, Kevin, and Matson. The long funeral procession led to a small memorial park where the neighborhood people were buried. About a hundred and fifty people gathered for the final prayers at the burial spot.

Ms. McDowell was embraced by dozens of well-wishers. When the ceremony was over, she walked to Mr. Pippin's car and got in, and the car disappeared down the winding road leading from the cemetery.

"Was a beautiful sendoff for the kid," Pop remarked as the Spain family headed for Jaris's Ford. "Pastor Bromley did a heckuva job. Pastor's wife, that Viola, she was good too. I figure Ms. McDowell knows how we all love her, especially the kids. I was proud of you carryin' the boy's casket, son. The hymns were good. That Amazin' Grace,' that's my favorite. And wasn't it beautiful that Oliver Randall, in his dark suit, sung solo with the praise chorus. That just grabbed my heart, you guys. Real good all the way, that service, real good."

"It meant so much to Ms. McDowell to see all you kids," Mom commented. "You're her life." Jaris squeezed his mother's hand.

CHAPTER EIGHT

The day after the funeral, Jaris and Amberlynn shared a shift at the Chicken Shack. She told Jaris the story of why Virgil Dunston shot Brandon and Shane. Virgil was working and going to night school. He'd never belonged to a gang or did drugs while he was a student at Lincoln High. His half brother, Buster Bennett, was clean too. Buster was outraged when he learned that his cousin, Zendon Corman, was dealing crack cocaine on Grant. Virgil knew his brother wouldn't have hesitated to turn them all in—Zendon and his partners, Shane and Brandon.

Zendon may have pulled the trigger on Buster, but Virgil blamed all three boys.

They were all part of the ugly crack cocaine business. Virgil figured that even if Shane and Brandon didn't actually agree with Zendon's decision to shoot Buster, they went along with it. The last straw for Virgil was when he heard the talk on the street. Shane and Brandon had busted out of jail and were selling crack again. He thought Buster had indeed died in vain. That's why Virgil Dunston turned murderer.

"Shane was the brother of my favorite teacher at Tubman," Jaris told Amberlynn. "Her family was troubled, but Ms. McDowell, she's the best."

Amberlynn was filling the plastic container with the cream packets for coffee. "It's a sad thing that happened," she remarked, half talking to herself. "The guys selling cocaine. It's like throwing a pebble in the water, and there's circle after circle spreading out. You don't harm just one person. The guy who killed Buster, those boys who hung with him, now they're dead, and Virgil's finished too. Imagine how Virgil's

137

mom feels. Her one son murdered and now her other son facing maybe life in prison. She's gotta feel like there's nothing worth living for anymore."

Jaris was grateful that Trevor and Kevin were also working that night. He needed his friends close. He was still feeling bad about what happened to Ms. McDowell's brother.

During a lull in the customer flow, Jaris made a comment. "Kinda surprised me how after the funeral Ms. McDowell left with Mr. Pippin. It's like he ushered her to his car and away they went."

"Oh, they go way back," Trevor responded. "My ma told me about that. I never knew before. Mr. Pippin's wife, she had Alzheimer's disease. She was in the nursin' home where Ma works. Mr. Pippin came in to see her every day. Mr. Pippin and his wife had this one daughter, and she had learnin' problems. Ms. McDowell was in college then, and she tutored kids with problems like that. She helped Mr. Pippin's daughter so much that he kinda bonded with her."

Trevor finished wiping down the counter and plopped the towel in the laundry hamper. "Then the wife died," he went on, "and the daughter got married and moved away. When Ms. McDowell was outta college and lookin' for a job, Mr. Pippin put in a good word for her. He got her hired at Tubman High. I bet when her and Mr. Pippin left the cemetery yesterday, they went to his daughter's house. Gives Ms. McDowell a nice friendly place to get away from it all."

"Wow!" Jaris exclaimed. "I never knew any of that. I always knew Mr. Pippin and Ms. McDowell were friendly to each other, but I didn't know the story, Trev. See how it goes? Paying it forward. Ms. McDowell helped Mr. Pippin's daughter when she needed it. Now Mr. Pippin is helping her, same as he helped her get the job at Tubman. That's what it's all about, man."

Kevin grinned wryly at Jaris. "There it is, man, your goody-two-shoes attitude is vindicated again."

"Right on!" Jaris laughed.

As the shift started getting busy, Jasmine and Marko came in for spicy chicken wings.

"Didn't see you guys at Shane Burgess's funeral," Jaris noted.

"He was no friend of mine," Marko declared. "Why should I go to a funeral for some bad dude who sold crack cocaine in the hood? Shouldn't have even had a funeral for him. Shoulda cremated him and dumped his ashes somewhere secret."

"Yeah," Jasmine agreed. "Somebody told me that a bunch of homies were there at the funeral, weird dudes in hoodies. Who wants to be a part of *that*?"

"I know. I saw them," Jaris conceded. "They were gangbangers. Everybody knew that, but funerals are not for the dude in the coffin. They're there to support those left behind. We wanted to show our support for Ms. McDowell. She's done so much for all of us."

"Yeah, man," Kevin said. "Didn't make no difference to Shane Burgess if we were there or not. But Ms. McDowell, she sure appreciated us being there."

"Anybody know where Brandon's funeral was?" Trevor asked. "I didn't hear anythin' about it."

"Cory and their parents had him cremated up in LA," Kevin answered. "They had something up there."

Marko looked around. "That fool Oliver come to the funeral, or he too busy fixin' up his dreadlocks?" he asked.

"Sure he came," Jaris said. "He was one of the pallbearers, and he sang with the praise chorus. He was good."

"This Sunday he gonna make a fool of himself again?" Marko asked.

"Oliver's gonna perform at some club downtown Sunday night," Jaris replied. "Me and Sereeta are going."

"Where's he comin' from anyway?" Marko grumbled. "He really think he's gonna be some famous idol or somethin'?"

"I think he will be," Jasmine remarked. "You can just feel the excitement when that boy steps on stage. I think he'll put Tubman High School on the map. It'll be like that guy who won that singin' contest on TV. He rode to the high school in a big parade and stuff. I seen pictures of him sitting in an open convertible. I bet we'll have a Oliver Randall Day at Tubman."

"Dream on, girl," Marko snapped. "He ain't goin' nowhere. He's what my ma calls 'a flash in the pan.' Everybody thinks it's cool now for that dude with the big voice to be doin' rock, but they'll get tired of him and wanna go on to the next thing. Anybody can fool people for a while."

Marko was desperate to impress Jasmine. He started making up a story. "I mean, like, just for fun, I went to this singing coach at Tubman Glee Club. I sang for him, and he said, if I was of a mind to, I could maybe sing—"

"Marko Lane!" Jasmine cried. "Give me a break. You sound like a coyote bayin' at the moon when you sing."

Kevin and Jaris looked at one another and hid their laughter behind a mutual attack of fake coughing.

"You can mock me, girl," Marko insisted. "But some of the most famous singers had really bad voices. You can't tell me this dude Bob Dylan had a great voice. He became a rock-and-roll icon, and still he didn't sound all that good. And what about that dude Joe Cocker."

"Who? Say what? Never heard of them. Marko, don't even think about it," Jasmine commanded. "I mean, you have embarrassed me enough. You better not start yowling like a sick tomcat sitting in the alley."

Marko looked angry. "Babe, just 'cause you're takin' that attitude, I got a good mind to get me some singin' lessons. You know that club where the amateurs come and sing on Tuesday nights—Artie's Abyss? I might just show up there and put Oliver Randall in the shade. He thinks he got a buzz goin', babe? I'll blow that place sky-high."

Jasmine covered her face with her hands. "Oh, you'd blow it, all right," she groaned.

"Why not, Marko?" Jaris asked. "We'll come, won't we, Kev?"

"Sure," Kevin agreed. "It should be good for some—" He stopped himself from saying "laughs," remembering he was a Chicken Shack employee and had to be polite. "Good for some entertainment," he said.

"See?" Marko crowed. "These two dudes, Jaris and Kevin, they don't even like me. But they're willin' to give me a listen. You're my chick, and you ain't standin' by me. What's wrong with you, girl?"

Marko and Jasmine walked out arguing. Kevin burst out laughing when they were out of sight. "Jaris, you don't know the best part of that story," Kevin explained, still laughing. "One time my grandparents got me to the Holiness Awakening Church for a wedding of somebody they knew. I forgot who was getting married. But Marko was

144

there with his mother. They musta known the bride or groom."

Kevin chuckled. "Anyway, the congregation started in singing, and Marko was right next to me. The sound comin' outta his throat reminded me of something. Then I figured out what it was. It was back in Texas when the old mule started brayin'!"

Trevor and Jaris laughed.

"I'm going to Artie's Abyss to hear him," Trevor announced. "Least we can do. We gotta support the Tubman High talent."

"Yeah, we can throw popcorn at him," Kevin suggested. Then he looked at Jaris. "You didn't hear me say that, dude."

"We gotta remember Marko's a hero," Jaris said. "We gotta remember what he did when he rescued Sereeta and that lady and her kids. Out of respect for that, we gotta be polite if we do show up at Artie's Abyss."

"Rats!" Kevin exclaimed. "Can we at least draw our fingers across our throats to get him to quit singing?"

"No!" Jaris commanded.

"But we can laugh a little," Trevor said. "Politely."

It was a good night. A lot of customers came in, and Jaris enjoyed the good-natured banter with his friends. Jaris, Trevor, and Amberlynn always got along fine, but Kevin added something special to the mix. He was sharp and funny and rebellious enough to keep things interesting.

Jaris was very glad he had followed his heart and hired Kevin. Kevin had been hanging with Cory Yates, and he was mad at the world. He was even suspected to be the guy who robbed the pizza place where he worked. Kevin even thought Jaris suspected him. Kevin was going downhill fast. He was out of luck and out of money. Mom and some of Jaris's friends warned him that Kevin's hot temper could cause trouble. Jaris had listened to that advice and hesitated. But Kevin needed the job so badly that Jaris hired him.

Hiring him had turned it all around for Kevin. Now Jaris hated to think what Kevin might have done if he hadn't gotten a break when he needed it the most. Maybe Kevin's whole future hung in the balance. And Kevin was working out even better than Jaris hoped. Kevin was curbing his temper, and he was a great counter person.

When Jaris got home from the Chicken Shack, he was surprised to see a light still burning in Chelsea's room. He rapped on her door, which was slightly ajar, and asked, "Hey, chili pepper, you still open?"

"Sure, come on in, Jaris," she answered. She was sitting on the edge of her bed with some pictures.

"What's that?" Jaris asked.

"We took some pictures at school with Athena's camera when we were back at Marian Anderson Middle School," Chelsea explained. "Old pictures of stuff that happened then." Chelsea didn't sound bubbly as she usually did, especially when she was looking at pictures. She sounded serious, almost sad.

Jaris sat on the bed beside his sister and looked at the pictures. He saw Chelsea,

Athena, and a boy making faces. They were sitting on the curb in front of Anderson, blowing bubbles from bottles and mugging.

Jaris's mouth turned dry. "Brandon, huh?"

"Yeah," Chelsea nodded. "You remember how mad you got when he was hanging around me? He was a freshman at Tubman and I was still in eighth grade."

"Uh-huh," Jaris said.

"He was pretty nice sometimes, Jare," Chelsea continued. "But his brother, he kinda led him into bad stuff. He looked up to his brother. He thought he was big stuff. But you know, Brandon was kinda fun. He was my ... first ... sorta boyfriend."

Jaris remembered Chelsea sneaking off to a party. She had told Mom and Pop that she was going to a girlfriend's house. Jaris followed her and found her at a party with Brandon and other unsavory characters. Jaris could the smell the liquor and grass. B.J. Brady, a big drug dealer, was even there. Since that time, B.J. had killed a man and died himself in a police chase.

Jaris had dragged Chelsea out of that party before she got into any real trouble. Their parents never found out. Chelsea promised she'd never do anything like that again. In exchange, Jaris promised to keep her secret. Both kept their word.

"I'm sorry he died like that, chili pepper," Jaris remarked.

"Yeah. Athena cried and cried," Chelsea confided. "He was the one who gave her that liquor when she passed out by the twenty-four-seven store. But she forgave him. He was so nice when he was nice that you could forgive him when he was bad, you know?" Chelsea's big eyes filled with tears.

Jaris put his arms around his sister and held her. In all the sorrow over Shane's death and the concern for Ms. McDowell, Jaris had forgotten Chelsea's loss. "I'm sorry, baby," he whispered to her.

"We called the Yates's house," Chelsea explained in a shaky voice, "Athena and me. We asked if there was gonna be a funeral for Brandon or anything, and they said no. They said he was cremated, and there wasn't any service. So Athena and me went and bought a bouquet of flowers and brought it to the Yates's house. We signed it. 'Love to Brandon, Athena Edson and Chelsea Spain.' "

Chelsea was staring at the pictures in her hands. "And the lady there—I guess Brandon's mom—she said they were going next week to throw Brandon's ashes in the ocean. She said they'd throw our flowers in at the same time."

"That was a nice thing you and Athena did, chili pepper," Jaris commented.

"I hope it didn't hurt him too much," Chelsea said.

"What?" Jaris asked.

"When he was shot," Chelsea replied. "Brandon was such a chicken about being hurt. One time we were skateboarding, and he scraped his knee. Me and Athena put on hydrogen peroxide, and he was almost crying. He didn't like to be hurt. So I hope it didn't hurt too much."

Jaris held his little sister a while longer. Then she gave him a hug and thanked him.

Jaris had forgotten about Chelsea's sorrow. He had been grieving for Ms. McDowell's terrible loss. But Chelsea was grieving for the boy who blew bubbles with her on the curb. To Jaris, Brandon Yates was a little punk, a threat to his precious sister. Now that Brandon was dead, the brash, sneaky punk seemed to disappear from his memory. He recalled only the grin on the boy's face and the boyish mischief in his eyes.

Jaris kissed Chelsea on the top of her head. "Goodnight, chili pepper," he said.

"Night, Jaris," she responded.

Jaris then noticed that Chelsea's favorite stuffed bear wasn't in its usual place on a high shelf. Chelsea had put it there when she became a freshman at Tubman High School. Tonight, the bear was on her pillow beside her.

"Goodnight, Silvertip," he said.

Chelsea's eyes grew wide. "You remembered his name!" she marveled.

Jaris smiled at his sister and turned out the light.

On Friday after school, the Tubman auditorium was empty. The janitors were cleaning up and were going to lock the doors in about an hour. A tall senior asked them if he could practice on stage until they came to finish up. They said sure, as long as he was gone by the time they left.

The boy had a guitar, but he wasn't a very good guitarist. He could strum but could not play a melody. The guitar was mostly a prop. The voice teacher had told the boy that he didn't have much range but that if he stuck to the lower notes, he might get by. Alone in the auditorium, the boy stood on the stage and began to sing.

Jaris was waiting for Chelsea to finish her math tutoring session and got bored sitting in his car. So he got out of the car and walked over to the vending machine. He bought an apple and munched on it as he walked around the campus to kill time.

Jaris was nearing the auditorium, and he tossed the apple core into a trash barrel. He was about to go back to his car when he heard a sound in the auditorium. At first, Jaris thought somebody was yelling for help. Jaris made a quick move toward the auditorium door—and then stopped short. The sound he heard was of somebody singing an old Beatles song, "Let It Be." That song had became famous way back when Grandma Jessie was a young woman.

But the guy singing it now wasn't doing it much good. Jaris peered through the open doorway. Marko Lane was on the stage, singing his heart out. Jaris quickly pulled his head back. He figured Marko was no singer, but this was way too much.

Jaris hurried away back to his car, snickering. He almost felt sorry for Marko Lane. Almost. Marko was desperately trying to impress Jasmine and get her mind off Oliver Randall's spectacular singing.

Jaris was glad Marko hadn't seen him peering through the doorway. Jaris didn't want to hurt him, even though Marko had hurt Jaris and Sereeta many times.

But especially on this day, Jaris didn't want to hurt anybody. One day, you're a little boy blowing bubbles and making funny faces on the curb. Not long afterward, you're shot dead in the street. So, Jaris thought, there has to be a stop to hurting anybody.

CHAPTER NINE

Sereeta and Jaris went to the little club on Sunday night to watch Oliver perform as Antar. Oliver's stage clothes were different for this gig. He wore a white, open-at-the-throat shirt, and he sang classics for the thirty-something crowd. The only teenagers in the club were Sereeta, Jaris, Kevin, and Carissa. Oliver belted out folk tunes that were written before he was born, when his father was young.

The audience loved him. Jaris heard people asking, "Who is that guy?" Oliver surprised the audience with his guitar, producing a biting sound, increasing in power to a growl. He did some old Richard Thompson songs, including "Dimming of the Day." The sad lyrics grabbed the audience, most of them hearing Thompson for the first time.

As the last notes of the set died in the air, the audience came alive, jumping up for a standing ovation. Everybody there seemed to realize they were witnessing a special performance.

Jaris didn't notice Alonee in the crowd until the show was over. She had been sitting toward the back of the room, staring at Oliver, her hands folded on her lap. Jaris and Sereeta approached her, and Jaris remarked, "He's amazing, huh?"

"He certainly amazes me," Alonee responded with a funny look on her face.

Jaris wanted to urge Alonee to treasure these precious moments. It was maybe the birth of a wonderful and rewarding career—or just a crazy, joyous interlude in their lives. Whatever it was, it was good.

He opened his mouth to speak when suddenly Alonee smiled and made an unexpected comment. "The scary part is I'm starting to like Antar almost as much as I like Oliver. That's the scary part. I didn't think I could love anybody as much as I love Oliver. Now he has a rival."

"Well," Sereeta laughed, "at least he lost the vest."

"Oh no," Alonee objected. "He's haunting the thrift stores for more of them." She giggled. "He's like a little boy wanting to dress up for Halloween or looking for new action figures to stick in the castle of doom."

Jaris and Sereeta walked outside into the darkness. They held hands as they walked to the parking lot and Jaris's Ford Focus.

On the way, Sereeta spoke. "Tomorrow after school, Mom and I are taking Jake to the park again."

Jake was Sereeta's half brother. He came along after Sereeta's mom and dad divorced, and her mom married another man.

"Mom's gonna pick me up from school, like she used to do when I was twelve," Sereeta went on. "Jake will be all buckled into his car seat, and we'll go down to the park and watch him discover bugs. Right now, ladybugs are his passion. His eyes get really big when he sees them."

Sereeta had been very jealous of the baby that her mother and stepfather were expecting. She spent half her time crying. Jaris remembered her mother's drinking problems and depression, but she was recovering from all that now.

"It might not always be this way," Sereeta remarked. "But me and Mom are really in a good place right now. We enjoy shopping. We laugh together. That's the best. When you can laugh with somebody, you're on top of the world. You know, what I do now is treasure every minute. You gotta love the good times while you have them. Grab life right now, and don't worry about tomorrow. Just be happy when you can."

The girl looked at Jaris and spoke with sincerity. "That's one of the things Ms. McDowell taught me. One of the *many* good things."

On Monday, everybody felt strange going to AP American History class. Ms. McDowell had taken the past three school days off, but now she was scheduled to be back. Jaris and his friends—the students closest to Ms. McDowell—agreed not bring up anything about the tragedy. They had gone to the funeral; they had hugged her and offered condolences on the hill above the gravesite. They had watched their teacher say good-bye to her baby brother.

But now it was Monday, and she was their teacher again. They owed it to her to remember that. Ms. McDowell walked in, dressed beautifully but professionally as always. She wore a pale blue suit and medium heels. She turned to the class and began her class: "Good morning."

The class greeted her in return.

"Who would like to begin and share some current research that has helped you with this project we are working on?" Ms. McDowell was back.

Oliver raised his hand. "I checked out Woodrow Wilson's *A History of the American People*, and it was an eye-opener for me. I've read a lot of biographies on Wilson, but this took me into Wilson's mind. I think the most poignant thing I ran across was his copy of the Treaty of Versailles and his scribbling on it. You could just feel the deep desperation he felt. The war had torn his soul. He so wanted this to be the last big war. He thought it all depended on this treaty, and it was going down to defeat in the Senate."

Oliver spoke as if he had spent the entire past week immersed in AP American History instead of rehearsing and performing as Antar. Jaris was in awe of him. Ms. McDowell turned to Jaris. He had to say something, but he was intimidated by Oliver's intelligence.

"I was studying President Wilson too," Jaris offered, "and I read this article he wrote after leaving office. It was in the *Atlantic Monthly*. In the article, he was almost begging for a world of sympathy and helpfulness, and the sad thing is, it didn't happen. World War Two was just around the corner."

Everybody in the AP class participated well. Ms. McDowell seemed her old self. She smiled now and then, raised her voice to emphasize a point, and looked a bit stern when someone made a misstatement. You would never have thought this was the same young woman weeping in the Holiness Awakening Church last Wednesday.

Jaris and Sereeta walked out together after class. "She's so great," Sereeta remarked. "She's a study in courage. Reminds me of something somebody wrote once, 'Facing it, always facing it—that's the way to get through. Face it.' "

"Joseph Conrad," Oliver said, coming up behind them.

"What?" Jaris asked.

"He wrote that. What Sereeta just quoted," Oliver explained.

"You make me sick, Oliver," Jaris groaned. "Did I ever tell you that?

You know too much. Do you know what happens to people who know too much?"

Alonee laughed and commented. "You know what's truly terrible about Oliver? He's right. That's what makes him so awful. Joseph Conrad did write that."

Oliver grinned amiably. "I found a black vest with sequins, Alonee. It's awesome. Those thrift shops are treasure troves!"

"He's crazy too," Alonee added. "That's another terrible thing about Oliver."

Marko Lane had been standing there. He heard Oliver talk about the black vest with the sequins. "You all set for Halloween, dude? Who you goin' trick-or-treatin' as— Dracula? Lissen up, man. I'm gonna be stealin' your thunder. I'm all set for talent night Tuesday at Artie's Abyss. Check it out. When people hear me, old Antar is gonna sink like a stone."

When Marko walked away, Kevin remarked to Jaris, "Say it ain't so, Joe. He's not really gonna sing in public."

"I heard him practicing in the auditorium," Jaris confided.

"So what do we do?" Trevor asked. "He's gonna be out on a limb. If we don't go, there'll be all strangers there, and they'll take the guy apart. Nobody's gonna be putting their hands together for poor old Marko."

"Like you think *we'll* be putting our hands together for 'poor old Marko'?" Kevin asked, grimacing.

"He's makin' Jasmine go," Jaris added. "And—oh man!—it's gonna be brutal. That's a nasty crowd down there anyway. I went there once. This poor guy, he was a ventriloquist with this hideous dummy, and they tore him apart. The guy was cryin'. I swear, he was cryin' like he was having a nervous breakdown."

"Ripe tomato time," Kevin declared. "Whose got a garden goin' bad right now so we can get a supply?"

"You guys," Denique Giles, Trevor's girlfriend, chimed in. "I haven't been at

Tubman long enough to know what problems you got with this guy. Give him a break. It won't kill us to go down there and act civilized."

"Here, here!" Trevor said.

"He was practicing 'Let It Be,' the old Beatles song," Jaris said.

"Oh brother! Not good," Oliver commented. "He needs to do something like rap. Yeah, just a lot of mixed-up, angry words to a beat. I mean, he's not gonna be Kanye West, but at least he won't be crooning. He could strut around on stage, looking mad and yelling out angry words. That could work. Marko is good at strutting."

"Whatever he does," Jaris announced, "we gotta go down there and show the flag, you guys. Denique is right. He's from Tubman. Think about it if he shows up down there and totally bombs. Everybody's gonna say, 'Look at the fool from Harriet Tubman High School.' They're gonna think our whole school's lame."

"Why doesn't Marko do a ventriloquist act, like that guy you saw, Jaris? Nobody'd know the difference between the dummy and Marko," Kevin remarked.

Carissa punched Kevin. "You're mean," she chided.

"It's part of my charm," Kevin replied.

Jaris found Jasmine walking alone after school and stopped her.

"Jaz," he told her, "I'm afraid Marko's gonna make a complete fool of himself Tuesday night at that joint."

"You're tellin' me?" Jasmine almost screamed. "I feel like whuppin' him upside his head. Maybe he'd be too woozy to perform."

"He was practicing the old Beatles song, 'Let It Be,' Jaz," Jaris said, "and it was ba-a-a-d."

"Ohhh!" Jasmine groaned.

"Jaz, listen," Jaris insisted, "we gotta get him to do some rap. One of these hip-hop songs with few lyrics and a lot of

165

yellin' and stomping around. Y'hear what I'm saying? Like 'Too Deep for Me.' You ever hear that? Guys complaining about the world falling apart. Marko could do that without embarrassing himself."

"Ya think?" Jasmine asked hopefully.

"Yeah, download it, Jasmine, and get Marko to practice it," Jaris urged.

"Jaris, why you bein' so nice?" Jasmine asked.

"Girl, I don't want the dude making the whole school look lame. Y'hear what I'm saying?" Jaris explained.

Chelsea and her friends went over to the Ice House for frozen yogurt after school. The kids had been saving their money, and seven of them piled into Mattie Archer's van. At the Ice House, they pushed a couple of tables together, sat down, and put in their orders.

Before long, Athena started talking about Brandon. "I can't believe he got shot like that," Athena remarked. "He wasn't a bad guy."

166

"He *was* bad, girl," Mattie Archer insisted. "He was dealin' crack cocaine. That's a killer right there."

"But it wasn't right to kill him like that," Athena objected.

"Yeah, you're right," Mattie Archer agreed. "Never right to kill nobody. But Brandon, he was goin' down the wrong road. Don't any o' you kids ever, *ever* even look down that road. Y'hear what I'm sayin'?"

"My dad says he'll beat me to a pulp if I ever use drugs," Heston chimed in.

"Good for your dad," Mattie responded.

"I tried grass once," Maurice confessed. "But I won't no more. I swear I won't."

"Me neither," Athena admitted. "I tried it once. I told my parents. They said never to do it again, but they didn't punish me or anything."

"Why'd he do it—that guy Virgil?" Maurice asked. "Why did he go shoot those dudes?"

"He had a little brother name o' Buster," Mattie Archer explained. "Zendon Corman killed Buster. Buster was gonna tell the cops Zendon was dealin' crack. Brandon and Shane, they were there too, helpin' Zendon deal crack. Virgil blamed them all for his little brother bein' dead. Virgil, he was burnin' with hate and vengeance, so he decided to get those boys. Now he's in jail, and he's gonna be there for the rest o' his natural life. Nobody come up a winner here."

"It's like war," Chelsea remarked. "One side kills your soldiers, and you kill their soldiers. My pop says we got war right on our streets."

"That's right, child," Mattie Archer agreed. "And the youngsters, they're the ones payin' the price. Four of 'em dead in just the past year. It's not right. They got their whole lives ahead of them, and then it's over."

Mattie Archer had ordered a strawberry yogurt, but she wasn't eating it. She looked right at the children around her, and she seemed about to cry as she went on. "They mighta done good things and made the

168

world a better place. But they never gonna get the chance, 'cause they dead."

"Pop says maybe we should bring in the army to help us," Chelsea commented. "He says it's too much for the cops. They try, but sometimes the gangs got better guns than they have. And people won't help them 'cause they're scared."

"I guess maybe that's a good idea," Mattie Archer responded.

"My father says it's the parents' fault," Inessa stated grimly. "The parents gotta watch their children, and they don't. They gotta watch them all the time and really punish them when they're bad."

"My pop sorta says that too," Chelsea admitted.

"Yeah," Keisha agreed. "I sorta lied a few weeks ago about where I was going when I went to your party, Athena. My parents grounded me, and they were really angry."

Athena shrugged her shoulders. "My parents trust me. I mean, they're not watching me all the time. Who wants parents looking over your shoulder every minute?"

"Better they lookin' over your shoulder than looking in your casket, baby," Mattie Archer advised. "Might be it comes down to that. These here are mean streets. You don't get no second chances, girl. You mess up, and that might be the end o' the line."

They all finished their frozen yogurts, and Mattie Archer took them all home. She dropped the kids at their homes except for Chelsea and Heston. Mrs. Archer dropped them back at Tubman, where they picked up their bikes for the ride home. They both loved to ride their bikes, and plenty of light was still in the sky.

"I like this time of day better than any other," Chelsea remarked as she unlocked her bike. "I like it when the sun has gone down, but it's still light. It's nice and cool, like the evening breeze is cool and soft. I love to ride my bike with the cool air sliding by."

"Yeah," Heston agreed, getting on his bike. He looked at Chelsea. She was so pretty. He loved the way the little curls framed her face. He loved her high cheekbones and the dimple in her chin. He thought she was just about the prettiest girl he'd ever seen. He thought she liked him a little bit, and he hoped she would go on liking him more and more as time went by.

As they rode down the street, Heston noted, "I seen a car at school, Chelsea, when we got dropped off. Just now, I looked back, and I seen the same car on the cross street."

"Did you see who was driving?" Chelsea asked.

"Some guy. I didn't see him good," Heston replied.

Chelsea felt a little nervous. With so many bad things going on, she didn't like the idea of some strange guy watching her and Heston.

"You think he was watching us, Heston?" Chelsea asked.

"I don't know. But when we got dropped off, he was there and then just now," Heston answered.

Chelsea pedaled a little faster, glancing back as she went.

"Chel," Heston said, "I'm gonna ride home with you, then go to my house. I don't like the idea of you going home alone."

Chelsea was really touched by Heston's protectiveness. She'd known he kind of liked her, but she hadn't thought he cared so much. The thought gave her goose bumps.

Heston saw the car one or twice again. When they got to Chelsea's house, Heston cried out. "There, Chelsea! There he is now. He just turned the corner!"

Chelsea stared at the car swinging out of sight around the corner. "The Ford Focus?" she gasped. *That's* the car that's been tailing us?"

"You know the guy?" Heston asked with a stern look on his face. "You better tell your pop that some older kid is following you around, girl."

"Heston," Chelsea cried, "that's my brother, Jaris."

"Huh?" Heston said. "Why would he be tailing us like that?" Heston was a little afraid of Jaris. He always tried to stay on Jaris's good side. Maurice Moore called Jaris a "maniac."

"Heston, he's worse than Pop," Chelsea explained. "He worries too. After the shootings, he told me last night that I shouldn't be riding my bike after dusk."

Jaris drove down the street and pulled into the driveway. "Hey, chili pepper. Hey, Heston," he said cheerfully.

"Jaris, were you spying on me?" Chelsea demanded. "Have you been playing cat and mouse with us?"

"Uh, I don't know what you're talking—" Jaris started to say. Then he grinned sheepishly. "I just wanted to know you got home safe, chili pepper."

Heston looked at Chelsea and told her, "If Brandon Yates had had a brother like him, he wouldn't be dead now."

CHAPTER TEN

On Tuesday night, Jaris and Sereeta arrived early at Artie's Abyss. Then Kevin came in with Carissa, and Derrick showed up with Destini. Oliver and Alonee arrived with Sami Archer and Matson Malloy. Trevor Jenkins and Denique Giles were the last of the gang to appear. They all took seats close to the front. They wanted to be able to set the tone for the audience. They figured that if they started clapping and cheering, then the catcalls and boos from the back of the place might be subdued.

The first performer was a slim blonde who sang a limp version of a Whitney Houston song. Jaris glanced over at Jasmine, sitting alone and looking tense and miserable.

Marko was already backstage, preparing for his performance.

As much as Jasmine and Marko fought, Jaris had no doubt that she loved him and he loved her. Jasmine would suffer if Marko was humiliated. She would rant and scream at him afterward for putting them through this, but her heart would ache for him.

A hip-hop group came on next, and they were pretty good and had a lively beat. Jaris hoped against hope that Jasmine had convinced Marko not to sing "Let It Be." That song highlighted all that was wrong with Marko. He had a poor voice, couldn't carry a tune, and completely lacked romantic charisma.

Finally, the shabby curtains parted again, and there was Marko Lane. He hesitated for a moment, and somebody behind him had to almost push him on stage. But Marko looked pretty good. He wore a close fitting black shirt and a lot of gold chains. He wore form-fitting black jeans. A few of the girls in the audience reacted with yells and whistles. At least Marko had his looks going for him. Most of the kids at Tubman High knew he could be a creep, but everyone agreed that he *was* handsome.

Marko had a guitar slung around his neck, but he really couldn't play it. Its main purpose was to give his shaking hands something to do. The weak house musicians started up, and Marko began to strut around the stage. He started growling out the lyrics to "Too Deep for Me." Jaris breathed a sigh of relief. He thought this might work.

Prices goin' up, wages goin' down,
Catchin' the despair that's goin' around,
Bad bad chick with another guy,
Goin' down for the count and that's
   no lie,
Losing my place in a dirty old world,
Just don't get it, maybe ought to die,
Too deep for me, I just can't see,
No place on earth for a dude like me.

Jaris grinned over at Jasmine with a thumbs-up.

176

Marko continued snarling his way through the rap lyrics, bopping around on stage like an angry black cat. It was easy to miss the fact that he had a terrible voice. Sometimes he sounded like a mean pit bull yelping and barking. At other times he sounded like a bad auto engine trying to start, but the rap song carried him.

When Marko finished his number, the Tubman kids loyally cheered, clapped, and stamped their feet. The audience probably would have applauded anyway for Marko's mediocre performance. But when all the others in the audience saw the ten teenagers up front applaud so loudly, they joined in. They figured they'd missed something and just went along.

Of the five contestants performing that night at Artie's Abyss, Marko Lane got the most applause, and he won for the night. He got a twenty-five-dollar gift certificate and a little trophy, a tiny guitar mounted on a chunk of fake marble. Jasmine was so happy, she cried. When Marko came into the audience, she threw her arms around him almost knocking him down.

"Girl," Marko complained, "you're puttin' on weight. You nearly decked me!"

"I am not, fool," Jasmine snapped back, but she was laughing.

"Y'see, dudes," Marko crowed as the Tubman students spilled outside into the darkness. "I'm as good as you are, Antar, or Oliver—whatever you wanna call yourself. I'm maybe gonna be a big rock-and-roll star before you, man."

Oliver smiled benignly, "Could be, Marko," he responded.

Everybody went across the street to a little coffee shop for lattes. Jaris couldn't remember when he and his friends got together with Marko and Jasmine like this. They had never been one big happy family. Usually when Jaris and his friends got together, they spent part of the time going over Marko's most recent creepy antics. The evening seemed surreal.

Jaris leaned over to Sereeta and said softly, "Babe, if we can all sit at the same table like this, maybe there *is* a chance for lasting world peace."

Sereeta leaned against Jaris and giggled.

Marko spent most of the time crowing about his performance, while Jaris and his friends concentrated on their lattes. Occasionally, Kevin looked like he couldn't take any more, and a murderous look came into his eyes. At one point, he looked as though he was about to dump his latte on Marko's head, but he resisted the impulse. Finally, Marko strutted off with a happy, giggling Jasmine on his arm. Before they went out the door, Jasmine looked back and winked cheerily at Jaris.

"A few more nights like this, and they can just lock me up in the nut house," Kevin declared. "I won't even protest."

"We did a good thing," Denique remarked. "Anybody can see the poor guy has as much singing talent as a screech owl, but we saved his pride."

Trevor grinned. "If you knew him like we do, Denique, you wouldn't be calling him the 'poor guy.' But you're right. We did a good thing."

"I almost killed him once," Kevin admitted. He was staring down at his latte and speaking very softly. "He was sayin' some awful things about me. So I was waiting for him, and I meant to beat him senseless. But then one of those weird, mystical things happened. My mom had been dead just a few months. Anyway, while I was waitin' to kill Marko, I heard her voice—she always called me 'Twister'—saying 'No, Twister, no.' She stopped me."

"I came close to whacking him too," Oliver added. "But then, Kevin, you grabbed my arm."

Jaris smiled. "I remember wanting to take a swing at him a couple of times myself."

"I'm proud of you guys," Alonee declared. "Tonight was your finest hour."

Everybody headed for their cars, which were parked outside Artie's Abyss.

"You know, Jaris," Sereeta commented as she buckled her seat belt. "I think Marko's changing. Not entirely, of course. But he's better than he used to be. I mean, don't you see it?"

"I guess so," Jaris admitted. "He does seem to be changing."

"People *can* change," Sereeta asserted with conviction. "We can't ever completely give up on them. My mom's changed. I haven't felt so happy with her since I was twelve years old. Maybe it won't always be that way, but at least I'll always have these happy memories."

Jaris dropped Sereeta off at her grandmother's house and got home himself. It was almost eleven, and he thought his whole family would be in bed. But they were all there in the living room. Jaris had the feeling he'd interrupted their conversation. They were looking at him, and everyone was smiling.

"Wassup?" Jaris asked.

Pop grinned. "Y'know what, Jaris? I didn't want to make a big deal of this, but I joined the BPA when I bought the garage. That's the Business Peoples Association. It's sorta like the neighborhood Chamber of Commerce. Everybody in the hood supposed to join up if they own a business. Some of 'em big muck-a-mucks and some of them little guys like me."

Jaris glanced at his mother. Her eyes were shining like stars.

"Anyways," Pop continued, "they give this prize to whatever business in the hood has increased their profits the most in the last quarter."

Chelsea could control herself no longer. "Pop won!" she screamed. "They're gonna honor him at a big lunch, and he gets a gold plaque and a thousand dollars. And we're all invited to the BPA dinner. Pop's gonna make a speech about how he got so successful!"

Jaris rushed over and gave his father a hug. "That's so great, Pop! Oh man, you beat out all the other businesses, Pop. That's, like, awesome!"

"Yeah," Pop responded. "That ol' garage is up twenty-five percent. I had to give them proof of that, all the records. So many beaters come in that we shot up in net profits like a rocket."

Pop's grin deepened. "And that ain't all. I been elected as one of the officers in the BPA, and I'm gonna encourage new businesses in the hood. There's a nice new restaurant opening up on Algonquin. It's a fancy place serving steak and seafood, that kind of thing. Lonnie Archer's brother is the owner there. So now we got a fancy-schmancy place to go for a special occasion. We don't have to be goin' all the way down to the Ye Olde Boathouse no more, or whatever. We can go right here to Archer's place. I talked them into having the big BPA luncheon right there. Be a shot in the arm to Leroy. He been workin' as a chef downtown, savin' his money, like me working for Jackson.

Now it's time for him to take care o' business."

The following day, Jaris heard his mother inviting Grandma Jessie to Pop's luncheon. Jaris could tell Mom was having a hard time. In the first place, she was trying to convince Grandma to come to a restaurant in their neighborhood. And the idea of a luncheon honoring Lorenzo Spain was probably hard for Grandma Jessie to accept.

Grandma didn't much care for Pop. She was very disappointed when her daughter married him. And she had been very opposed to Pop taking out a loan against the house to buy the garage. She didn't expect him to succeed. In fact, she predicted he would fail and ruin the family's finances. Winning the award was a slap in her face.

"Mom, you've got to come," Mom insisted. "It's an important family event.

Chelsea and Jaris are so excited. They insisted that you be there."

Jaris winced. He and his sister would have preferred Grandma to stay home. It wasn't easy to hear your mother lie, but he didn't blame her. Mom had to use all the weapons she had.

"The kids would just be so disappointed if you didn't come, Mom," Jaris's mother went on. "And you know, this new restaurant is beautiful. It's the very first nice restaurant in this neighborhood, and it means so much to all of us. Now we have somewhere nice close by to go to for special occasions."

A note of distress entered Mom's voice. "No, Mom, it's not anywhere near Grant. There are nice condos on Algonquin. No, there's no graffiti there. Honest, Mom."

Then suddenly, Jaris heard a lilt in Mom's voice. "You will? Oh, that's wonderful. Just wait till I tell the kids. They'll be so happy. They were so worried you wouldn't come."

Jaris winced again. Poor Mom probably had done more lying this morning than she'd done in her entire life.

As the Spain family entered the restaurant on the day of the luncheon, Pop was seated at the front table with the other BPA board members. The Spains took the table set aside for them at the head of the room.

Kobe Myers, one of Mr. Myers's sons, who was recently back from serving in the Middle East, announced his good news. He was buying the old pizza parlor and refurbishing it. He was turning it into a family restaurant and low-cost catering hall. Everyone applauded.

Al Sedgewick, who owned the supermarket and was president of the BPA, announced plans to expand the market. Again there was applause. Sedgewick then introduced the new members of the BPA's governing board: Leroy Archer, Kobe Myers, and Lorenzo Spain.

When Pop's name was announced, Mom applauded vigorously. Although Grandma Jessie put her hands together, they made no sound. Jaris and Chelsea were so happy for Pop that they didn't care how sour Grandma looked. When Pop was given the beautiful plaque and thousand-dollar check, Pop got up to say a few words.

"It's the old story we all knew since we were kids," Pop began. "You gotta believe in yourself. You gotta work hard. You gotta face down challenges. And if you get knocked down, you gotta get up again and keep on facing it. You gotta treat your customers right. They're good people, struggling same as you. And sometimes you gotta cut 'em a break, and they'll remember that and be loyal."

Pop turned toward his family. "And you gotta have a family like mine, a wife like my Monica. She was worried sick when we took on the new financial responsibilities of a business, but she stuck with me anyway. And kids like my Chelsea and Jaris. They make me proud of makin' the world a better place by sendin' off kids like that into the future."

For a moment, Mom looked concerned that Pop wouldn't mention Grandma— or worse, say something mean. But Pop flashed a big grin and continued. "And that fine upstandin' lady, Jessie Clymer. She's my mother-in-law and always ready to give me her best advice, whether I wanna hear it or not. She always willin' to tell me what she thinks." A few quiet snickers rippled through the room. Grandma Jessie was staring at the wall as Pop spoke.

"How could I go wrong with a team like that behind me?" Pop sat down to thundering applause and not a little laughter. Grandma Jessie now stared at him, not quite sure whether she should feel honored or insulted.

Later that day Jaris picked up Sereeta, and they went to the beach. Oliver Randall was throwing a party for his friends. They arrived just after dusk with the harvest moon bigger than anybody could ever remember seeing it.

Everybody from Alonee's posse was there. Kevin and Carissa, Derrick and Destini, Trevor and Denique, Sami and Matson, Oliver and Alonee. They spread beach blankets on the sand, ate hot dogs and hamburgers, and washed it all down with sodas.

"It was so good to see Pop honored today," Jaris remarked. "He's had his share of disappointments in his life, but he's worked so hard. For him to get recognized like this, man, it made me so happy."

Sereeta smiled and gave Jaris a hug.

"I'm so happy right now, it's almost scary," Jaris commented.

Sereeta rested her head on his shoulder and said, "Yeah, I know, me too."

In his wildest dreams, Jaris had never dreamed there would be a night like this, with this girl beside him. Jaris and Sereeta sat side by side, hands clasped.

"I'm gonna get credit for AP American History now for sure," Jaris told her. "I was worried about that."

"Me too," Sereeta responded. "I'm okay too."

"I knew you'd ace it, babe," Jaris said.

"Before you know it, we'll be graduating and going off to college," Sereeta commented.

"Babe, I hope you know that through all the ups and downs, you were the one who kept me sane," Jaris told her.

"Likewise," Sereeta replied, giggling.

Only a short distance away, Oliver Randall was sitting with Alonee. He was wearing a T-shirt and shorts, and he looked like his old self. He didn't look like Antar.

"I wonder where we'll be next year at this time," Alonee mused.

"I don't know, babe," Oliver responded.

"I thought we'd be at college but . . ." Her voice trailed off.

"Alonee," Oliver told her in a suddenly insecure voice, "whatever happens, I want to know you're on my side."

"Babe," Alonee sighed, "you're ready to toss away all your plans—*our plans.*

You're ready to throw them up in the air and let the wind decide the future. And now you're saying I should go along for the adventure."

"A ship in the harbor is safe, Alonee, but that's not what ships are for," Oliver said.

Alonee looked up into the sky. It looked wondrously mysterious and bright.

"I guess we could take a year off after graduation," Alonee suggested in a trembling voice. "A lotta people do that."

Oliver leaned over, took Alonee into his arms, and held her tightly against him.

Silence followed, except for the pounding of the waves and the rush of the wind, salty and cool. The kids in the posse sat there in pairs, hands clasped, heads on one another's shoulders. They were lost in their thoughts about the future.

For all of them, the future was like the black ocean that melted into the dark horizon. For all the kids on the beach, the future was not as certain as it had been not long ago. They'd witnessed Oliver's life changing dramatically. They all wondered whether he'd be a college student next year—or a rock singer. Alonee wondered whether she and Oliver would still be together.

And the kids had seen more than one future shattered with the pop-pop-pop of a handgun. Virgil Dunston had shot Brandon Yates and Shane Burgess. They had no future on this earth anymore. Dunston threw away his own future; he'd be spending the rest of his life in prison. And he took away any future that Ms. McDowell might have wanted to spend with her brother.

If things could change so quickly and so much, could anyone be sure of what was to come?

The dark waves crashed on the sand not far from where the kids sat but could not reach them. For now, they were safe. But soon, the future—in whatever form it took—would be upon them. And they would all have to face it.